Zoltar's eyes grew bright red. His head began to bob hypnotically.

A sign inside the booth lit up: AIM RAMP TOWARD ZOLTAR'S MOUTH. Josh fiddled with the controls on the front of the booth until the end of the ramp was poised just over Zoltar's mouth. Another sign lit up: ZOLTAR SAYS MAKE YOUR WISH.

"Make your wish . . . right," Josh mumbled, concentrating on the controls. "Okay, then . . ." —he closed his eyes—"I wish I were big . . ."

Josh stepped back from the controls studying the machine. Then he noticed its electrical cord dangling from its side. He grabbed the middle of the cord. It turned out to be frayed, glints of copper showing through its fabric insulation. . . .

Josh dropped it and turned to look up at Zoltar. The red eyes continued to glow eerily, the head to nod in empty agreement.

There was a faint whirring sound as the end of an oblong of cardboard ejected from a slot next to the coin release button. Josh extracted the card and read from it.

YOUR WISH IS GRANTED

big™

B.B. Hiller and Neil W. Hiller

BALLANTINE BOOKS • NEW YORK

This one is for Elaine Molkentine and Joan Stilwell.

—B. B. Hiller
—Neil W. Hiller

CHAPTER 1

THE message was clear: if Josh Baskin didn't react quickly, it was all over for him.

He was trapped in the incandescent blue cavern of the evil Ice Wizard, now facing his powerful nemesis alone. The rock floor around the adventurer was strewn with the twisted carcasses of slain ice dwarfs, icicles already forming on their stringy white beards. Josh warily regarded his implacable foe from behind a protecting boulder. The Wizard was poised high above the cavern floor atop a pillar, pointing his death-dealing sceptre toward his cowering adversary.

"MELT WIZARD," Josh keyed into the computer.

"WHAT DO YOU WANT TO MELT THE WIZARD WITH?" immediately appeared on the screen.

It was such a dumb response that it sheared Josh's concentration. He threw his head and shoulders back and glared up at the ceiling as if expecting to see some considerably more intelligent message written there. What he saw instead were his model airplanes suspended above him by transparent fishing line.

Wasting precious seconds, Josh spread his arms, palms up, and returned his gaze to the video screen. "What do you *think* I want to melt him with?" he implored it instead of entering his answer on the keyboard.

The walkie-talkie lying on the lower bunk of his bed, smothered beneath yesterday's jeans, momentarily rasped static as if in response. He flinched and tore his eyes from the monitor to glance at the radio in annoyance. As he turned back to the screen, he got a fleeting view of Don Mattingly's expression on the poster on his bedroom door. The Yankee first baseman seemed to grin in anticipation of the obvious decisive blow Josh was about to deliver. . . .

"Jo-osh . . ." his mother shouted from the foot of the stairs. "Josh, I told you to take out the garbage."

"In a minute," he called out in return, not meaning it, while rapidly sealing the fate of the Ice Wizard at the keyboard.

"THROW . . . THERMAL . . . POD . . ."

"Jo-osh. I'm not going to tell you again," a sing-song reminder wafted up from the kitchen.

"Good," Josh muttered quietly. "Just a second,

Mom," he called aloud as the response to his strate-gem appeared on the screen.

"Joshua Baskin . . ."

"YOUR HESITANCY HAS COST YOU DEARLY."

"Tell me about it," Josh said sourly.

"THE WIZARD, SENSING YOUR APPREHENSION, UN-LEASHES A FATAL BOLT FROM THE ICE SCEPTRE, FREEZ-ING YOU INTO OBLIVION. WITH LUCK, YOU WILL THAW IN SEVERAL MILLION YEARS."

"Terrific," Josh said softly. "At least they won't be able to make me take out the garbage."

Josh sighed, shut off his computer, pushed back his chair, and rose. He ran his fingers through his curly brown hair and turned to leave. His head missed col-liding with his model airplanes by several inches. Aside from Rachel, his one-year-old sister, Josh was the only person he knew who *never* hit his head on those planes. He sighed once again. Being twelve had some real drawbacks. Being shorter than most of his friends and taking out the garbage instead of killing evil wizards were just two of them. He didn't think his birthday in a few weeks was going to help.

Josh extracted his navy-blue New York Yankees warmup jacket from the jumble of clothing on the lower bunk, glanced at Mattingly on the door as if looking for a sign of kinship, and left his room.

As Josh noisily descended the stairs to the kitchen, he became more philosophical about the Wizard de-bacle. He was meeting his next-door neighbor and best friend, Billy Kopeche, at the school grounds to shoot some baskets. Might as well haul the garbage on the way out. His mother had actually *helped* him to be on time by truncating his adventure.

Mrs. Baskin was scrubbing the sink when Josh entered the kitchen. Evidence of Saturday-morning cleaning was scattered around the room. A broom leaned against the refrigerator; soap and cleanser bottles were distributed on the counter and table; and three large plastic garbage bags were lined up in the middle of the room. Rachel skittered and bounced around the kitchen floor in her walker, now gleefully crashing into a garbage bag and waving the teething ring clutched in her chubby hand in triumph. She beamed up at Josh for approval of her feat.

Mrs. Baskin's brown hair was tied back with a scarf. She looked wearied from her housekeeping efforts as she turned from the sink, pushing a stray strand of hair back with her forearm.

"Those three," she announced, pointing with her extended forefinger at the offending garbage bags, as if about to freeze them into oblivion for several million years. She turned back to the sink.

Josh approached his sister, bent over her, returning her smile, and snatched the teething ring from her hand. Rachel let out a wail and bounced up and down unhappily, running the bumper of her walker into his shin in the process.

"Give it back to her," his mother ordered without turning. He stared at the toy in his hand. It was just about the right size and shape for a thermal pod. . . .

In Josh's mind, the kitchen became suffused with an incandescent blue glow. He cocked his wrist for the short throw of the incendiary device to the sink.

His mother turned toward him, wiping her hands with a paper towel. Deftly, Josh shifted directions, scooped his arm around, and handed off the toy to Rachel. "Now drive the lane for the lay-up basket," he urged.

"Josh, you should be nice to her. She's your sister."

"Sure, Mom." He stooped to give Rachel a kiss on the forehead, above the cereal stains. She whooped and smacked him in the eye with her drool-covered toy. "And she's a truly wonderful one, too." He rose, hefted two of the plastic bags over his shoulder, Santa-style, and fumbled out the back door with them, dragging the third.

Josh crushed the final plastic bag into the can next to the garage and stooped to pick up the lid from the ground. Suddenly alert to danger, he spun swiftly and used the Impervious Shield to ward off the final ambush volleys of death rays emanating from across the yard. Wham. Zap. Ping.

Satisfied, he turned, replaced the lid, and sauntered away as if nothing had happened. It was almost time to meet up with Billy. He jumped onto his bicycle, pushed off down the driveway, and was about to reach down and toggle on the afterburners when his escape was interrupted by his father's voice from behind him.

"Finish your homework?" his father called, emerging from the garage, wiping his hands on a rag.

Josh slowed. "It's Saturday," he informed Mr. Baskin over his shoulder.

"And tomorrow's the carnival," his father reminded him.

Josh stopped. The carnival came to town once a year. It boasted scary rides, a midway with games where you could win neat things, a fun house, and food from all the major food groups: the popcorn and peanuts group; the cotton candy and taffy apple group; the hot dog and burger group. Everybody went, including Cynthia Benson. Josh felt a wave of . . . something.

"But Dad," he protested, turning his bike and retracing his way up the driveway, the battle already lost.

"You want to go tomorrow night?" his father asked.

"Can I go by myself?" he asked hopefully.

"No."

That was another drawback to being twelve. He was old enough to take out the garbage by himself, but he couldn't do anything *fun* without his parents around.

"Can't I do *anything* alone?" he pleaded.

"Sure. You can go up and do your homework." His dad grinned, then added with a smile as if cooing to Rachel: "All by yourself."

Josh marched his bicycle around the corner, leaned it against the house, and stormed in, letting the kitchen door slam loudly behind him in protest.

Josh was in such a hurry to finish his own homework that he hadn't had time to complete Billy Kopeche's math. Now riding toward the basketball court on the playground, where Josh could see Billy elaborately imitating a shrunken Larry Bird, Josh rehearsed what he would tell his friend about the math.

As he frequently reminded Josh, Billy Kopeche had been born a full three months before his friend. The reminders had come particularly frequently near the time of Billy's August birthday celebration. This age disparity gave Billy an unfair advantage over his younger friend. It was even worse, from Josh's viewpoint, than the fact that Billy was also the taller, by six inches. At least Josh had a hope of one day growing taller than Billy. He could never *hope* to be older.

Or so he thought.

Billy wore his hair in a compromise between real punk and what the rules at George Washington Junior High School permitted: short and choppy on the top, longish and straggly on the sides and over his forehead. His face reminded Josh of his sister Rachel's: angelic in repose, and belying an inner toughness. He did not share this observation with Billy.

Today Billy sported his favorite tie-dyed sweatshirt under a denim jacket festooned with badges and military campaign ribbons. Billy cavorted around the court in his nondesigner sneakers (both laces untied), Billy's down-market emblems of his nonconformism.

"Game of HORSE?" Billy called out as Josh approached and dismounted his bicycle, leaning it against the fence. Josh nodded. Billy dribbled the ball toward him, spun, and sank a jump shot from the corner of the court. He raised his arm in triumph. Josh walked over to him and gave him a high five.

"Where've you been?" Billy called over his shoulder, retrieving the ball and smartly snapping a two-handed pass over to Josh. Josh stood in the same spot and attempted to duplicate Billy's shot. He missed. "You got an *H*," Billy announced. "What kept you?"

"Guess."

Billy stood at the free-throw line and pumped in a short jumper. "You do my math, too?"

Josh picked up the ball, moved to the spot, missed again. "Not yet."

Billy took the rebound. "That's an *O*." He hooked in a short shot from the right of the basket. "Josh, you were supposed to do my math."

"You sound just like my mom and dad," Josh said, attempting the hook. "*R*, damn it. I'll have it for you tonight, okay?"

"It's just that I bet Bobby Feinberg," Billy said from the top of the key, his back to the basket. He launched the ball backward over his head. It arced through the air and dropped noiselessly through the hoop.

Josh gawked at his friend, who grinned back matter-of-factly. "*S,E*. I give up." He paused. "*What* did you bet Bobby Feinberg?"

"I bet him I'd get an A." He studied Josh. "You want to get a burger?" he added hurriedly.

"You're crazy," Billy announced to Josh a few minutes later en route to The Burger Box. They were strolling down Front Street, idly window-shopping in the stores along the sidewalk. Billy was dragging his skateboard, Josh walking his bike. Billy tossed the skateboard aside and, watching his reflection in a store window to make sure he got the motion right, wound up, kicked his left leg high, and imitated a pitcher's delivery for Josh, complete with a smart follow-through, readying him to field a comebacker. "Tekulve's a submariner," he pronounced, gesturing to the window as if it contained evidence.

"He is not." Josh locked his bike into the stand at the curb, then performed his own version of the pitcher's motion. "He comes sidearm, like this," he said, finishing the delivery.

"*That's* not sidearm," Billy protested. "That's sort of underhanded—just like Tekulve's."

"It ain't," Josh declared.

"It is so. *This* is sidearm." Billy executed another mime, watched the pitch, and announced, ". . . Annnd . . . he *gets* him. . . ." He turned to Josh. "See?" He retrieved his skateboard.

They continued down the street toward The Burger Box. As they approached the local hangout, they saw that the sidewalk in front of the entrance was, as usual, crowded with their classmates and friends. Josh stopped dead. Cynthia Benson was among the group lounging near a parking meter. To Josh she represented all the fascinating, inaccessible beauty of an older woman. She was fifteen. Her blonde hair shone in the fall sunlight, glistening. Her cheeks glowed from the slight chill in the air, and her blue eyes sparkled with animation.

Josh was transfixed.

"How'd a geek like Freddy Benson get a big sister like that?" Billy wondered, following Josh's frozen stare.

"Beats me," Josh mumbled.

Billy shrugged and began pushing his way deftly through the crowd. Josh tore his eyes from Cynthia and followed on rubber legs.

He heard the words: "Hi, Josh." He turned to see their source.

It was unmistakably Cynthia saying hi to *him*.

Then she smiled and a sea wave broke under his heart.

Billy glanced from Cynthia to his mesmerized friend and responded airily on Josh's behalf. "Hi."

Josh remained frozen in the doorway as Cynthia and her friends turned to walk down the block. Billy called after her, pointing purposively to Josh's head. "He says hello!"

Cynthia smiled enigmatically over her shoulder. Billy ducked around Josh to stand in front of him, waving his hand before Josh's eyes to break the spell. "Un-be-lievable!" Billy intoned.

That evening, the usual confusion reigned in the Kopeche kitchen. Billy, his mother, and his three older brothers and sisters were ready for supper. Mrs. Kopeche sat at an end of the Formica table, complaining. "I'm a person. I'm not your maid. Can any of you appreciate that?" Mrs. Kopeche asked.

Billy took a platter of meat loaf from the oven and set it on the table.

"You waltz through here . . . ." Mrs. Kopeche continued, ". . . like it's some kind of resort—lounging around, waiting for your dinner to be cooked, your clothes to be ironed."

Billy emptied a pan of potatoes onto a platter, took a serving spoon from a drawer, and carried them to the table.

"What about me?" Mrs. Kopeche wailed. "Have you ever just once thought about how *I* feel?"

At the stove, Billy dumped the pot of vegetables into a bowl.

"Do you know what it's like to work eight hours and come home to this?" She slammed her fist on the table for emphasis. The plates and silverware jumped. "Every. Single. Day." No one looked up to answer her.

Silently, Billy placed the bowl of vegetables on the table, near his mother's hand. He turned back to the counter.

"None of you ever offers to help me! Why?" she asked.

Billy took a plate from the cupboard, walked to the table, and sat down.

"I can't do it anymore," Mrs. Kopeche announced.

Billy speared a slice of meat loaf and slid it onto his plate. He spooned some potatoes and vegetables around it.

"I just can't," Mrs. Kopeche said, lowering her head to her arms crossed on the table.

Billy rose, picked up his plate and silverware, and silently left the room.

Later that evening, Josh and Billy held their nightly confab over their walkie-talkies. In the top bunk in his room, Josh gripped his radio in his left hand and a flashlight in his right, aiming the beam out his window and through Billy's window in the Kopeche house, across the driveway. They were playing tag.

"Tell me," Josh whispered into the walkie-talkie.

"First the math," Billy insisted.

"I'll *give* you the math, Billy. Now, what's going on?"

"You're in," Billy responded dramatically.

"What do you mean—I'm *in*?"

"Cynthia Benson."

Josh sat up. "What about Cynthia Benson?"

"Are you ready for this?" Billy paused dramatically. "She doesn't like Barry anymore."

The beam of Billy's flashlight zigged and zagged across Josh's ceiling. Josh's head crashed back down to the pillow on his bunk. He halfheartedly tried to catch Billy's beam with his own as the import of his friend's words sunk in. "So . . ." Josh managed to respond nonchalantly.

Billy's beam disappeared from the ceiling. "Waddaya mean *so . . .*? That's it. She's *available*."

"Billy, just 'cause she doesn't like Barry anymore . . ."

"Jo-osh," his mother intoned as she opened the door to his room. Josh snapped off his flashlight and plunged the radio under the covers. "It's after midnight," his mother informed him. "You should have been asleep a long time ago."

"I am asleep, Mom," Josh responded drowsily.

"Of course you are. Now, say good night to Billy." His mother pulled the bedroom door closed.

Josh pulled the radio from beneath the covers. "I got to go, Billy," he hissed.

A wet kissing sound came over the radio in response. Josh stared at it in disbelief. "Sweet dreams," Billy said.

CHAPTER 2

THE smell of popcorn and grilled sausage and sawdust wafted together on the fall air. The steady murmur of the crowd churning along the midway competed with the canned calliope music blasting from the huge speakers at the epicenter of the carousel, the steady *brinnng, brinnng, bringgg* of the games in the arcade tent, the shouts of the motley-clad barkers in the game booths.

Shadeless light bulbs strung from bare four-by-fours temporarily driven into the ground as stanchions transformed what had been an empty meadow into a scene of magic and mystery and excitement. Powerful searchlights at the end of the midway, diesel generators throbbing, probed the starlit sky. They directed the eye upward, toward the whirling multicolored lights of the Ferris wheel towering above the hubbub.

And to the Avenger.

Josh gazed at the quadrant of the sky where metal cages full of shrieking captives dangled from the massive mechanical arms of the Colossus of the Midway, the Apotheosis of Adventure, the Ride That Separates the Men from the Boys. . . .

No way was he going to go up on that thing.

Rachel gurgled happily from her vantage point over her mother's shoulder. Mrs. Baskin shifted the baby to her other arm. "I don't know, Bob," she said to Josh's father.

"He's a big boy, Carol," he replied. Tearing an orange ticket from the strip in his hand and giving it to Josh, he confided to his son, "Sport, you don't have to go on it if you don't feel like it."

Josh took the ticket from his father and escaped in the direction of the Ferris wheel. But as he passed the line for the Avenger, he found a familiar face in the crowd. "Omigod," he intoned wonderingly.

It was Cynthia Benson *alone* at the end of the Avenger line.

He skidded to a halt and, swallowing his fear, sauntered over to where Cynthia was gazing up at the Avenger. He quickly formulated a clever greeting and cleared his throat.

"Hi," he said, too loud.

"Oh, hi, Josh," Cynthia replied, surprise in her voice.

Having used his entire small-talk repertoire, Josh studied their surroundings for inspiration.

"Are you here alone?" Cynthia offered. She was *talking* to him.

"Yes," he managed. Then: "Definitely."

"Look." She pointed down the midway. "Aren't those your parents?"

Josh glanced at the crowd. "Where?" he asked in panic.

"Right over there." she said.

To his dismay, Josh saw his family at a nearby candy stand. Both his parents *waved*.

"Yeah, I guess they are here," he said, surprise in his voice.

She regarded him through narrowed eyes. "Have you been on this before?" she asked, pointing to the Avenger.

"This one?" Josh asked casually. "Oh, sure," he said. "Lots."

"Is it scary?"

He looked up at it and shrugged. "Nah," he assured her. "Definitely," he said under his breath.

A deep voice boomed behind him. "Who's this?" the voice demanded.

Josh turned to see a strapping sixteen-year-old boy in a team jacket emblazoned with varsity letters, carrying two ice cream cones. The boy handed one to Cynthia, who smiled warmly in thanks. She wrapped her arm around his waist.

"This is Josh Baskin." She pointed to him with the ice cream cone.

"How ya doing?" the older boy asked cheerfully, obviously unthreatened by Josh's presence. It didn't do anything for Josh's now badly shaken self-esteem.

Josh managed an acknowledging nod.

"This is Derek," Cynthia explained. "He drives."

Derrick? Josh wondered. The guy looked like a derrick, since he was about eight feet tall.

"Next!" called the ticket taker at the head of the line. The color drained from Josh's face. His feet were frozen in place. "Yo! Next, please!" It was even louder this time. It was Josh's turn.

"Go ahead, kid," Derek told him.

Josh swallowed his fear, strode up to the ticket taker, and handed him the sweaty orange cardboard as he marched through the gate to his doom.

"Sorry, kid," the ticket taker said, returning Josh's ticket.

"What?" Josh asked, looking up, confused.

The man pointed to a sign next to the turnstile. YOU MUST BE AT LEAST THIS TALL TO RIDE THE AVENGER, it read over a black line several inches above Josh's eye level.

"Come on, kid. You're holding up the line." He dismissed Josh with a wave.

Being short was one thing—but being short in front of Cynthia was another altogether. Stunned and humiliated, Josh studied the ground as he stumbled back toward the end of the line and the midway.

"Well, it's a stupid rule," he heard Cynthia say from what seemed a vast distance as she and Derek passed through the turnstile. "See you, Josh," she called after him.

Josh turned and affected a smile that came out as a grimace. But Cynthia and Derek were already disappearing up the ramp into the ride. Josh slam-dunked his ticket into a litter drum, kicked the receptacle for good measure, jammed his hands into his pockets, and slouched dejectedly up the midway.

What good was a ticket if they wouldn't let him ride? What difference could a couple of inches—well, four or five—make about riding the Avenger, anyway? Why did they have to embarrass him in front of Cynthia Benson—of all the people in the world—and her car-driving derrick? He stormed up the dirt road through the carnival, his feet a mortal threat to every clod and paper cup appearing in his path.

Then he was alone in the dark near the Hudson River. He leaned on the railing and studied the water as it swirled and eddied, languid and restless, like an ocean of black oil.

A noise behind him, perhaps the wind, startled Josh. He whirled. There, beyond the crowd and noise from the carnival, was an isolated wood and glass booth bathed in the soft multicolored glow of the lights from the midway. Josh approached it slowly. The calliope played vaguely in the background.

ZOLTAR SPEAKS, the sign on the booth read. While it was clearly a relative of the arcade games Josh was familiar with, the booth looked old-fashioned to him. Its elaborate wooden trim was carved and scalloped. There were worn brass control wheels on the front panel. A long metal ramp mounted in the ceiling extended toward the mouth of a plaster gypsy.

Zoltar himself was really just a plaster head and shoulders ensconced behind glass panels in the top half of the booth. He had muttonchop whiskers and an empty stare in eyes that were too big. His mouth gaped like that of a feeding fish with a lantern jaw. The figure's turbaned head leaned backward at a crazy angle in a high Ming the Merciless collar. The dusty material of Zoltar's gown was a bottle-green and regal purple brocade.

Josh shivered. He read the small sign between the control handles of the game: INSERT COIN TO TOP OF RAMP.

Josh fished a quarter from his pocket. The booth had no screen on which to display instructions, but it was clear from the height of the coin slot, the shape of the ramp, and Zoltar's mouth—and the pile of coins around his stiff torso—that the object of the game was to get Zoltar to swallow a coin.

Josh reached up and dropped his quarter into the slot above his head. Nothing happened.

He hit the heel of his hand against the side of the booth. Still nothing happened.

Suddenly, in a fury, the frustrating and humiliating events of the evening caught up with Josh. He flailed at the sides of the booth with his fists and kicked it with his feet. He stopped, spent.

Zoltar's eyes grew bright red. His head began to bob hypnotically.

A sign inside the booth lit up: AIM RAMP TOWARD ZOLTAR'S MOUTH. Josh fiddled with the controls on the front of the booth until the end of the ramp was poised just over Zoltar's mouth. Another sign lit up: ZOLTAR SAYS MAKE YOUR WISH.

"Make your wish . . . right," Josh mumbled, concentrating on the controls. "Okay, then . . ." He closed his eyes. "I wish I were big."

A third sign glowed: PRESS BUTTON TO RELEASE COIN. Josh made a final adjustment of the controls and pushed the button between them.

The coin wobbled down the rail, seemed to dangle, then fell off its end and into Zoltar's mouth. The jaws closed on the coin.

Josh stepped back from the controls, studying the machine. Then he noticed its electrical cord dangling from its side. He grabbed the middle of the cord. It turned out to be frayed, glints of copper showing through its fabric insulation.

A plug dangled from the end of the wire.

Josh dropped it and turned to look up at Zoltar. The red eyes continued to glow eerily, the head to nod in empty agreement.

There was a faint whirring sound as the end of an oblong of cardboard ejected from a slot next to the coin-release button. Josh extracted the card and read from it.

YOUR WISH IS GRANTED

CHAPTER 3

THE storm began at midnight. A sudden gust of wind whipped across the Baskin yard, tearing leaves from the branches and churning them into whirlwinds that clattered against the garage. The wind billowed around Josh's bike, lofting it to crash against the tree in the front yard of the house. The fence gate swung wildly, first open, pounding against the picket fence, then closed, slamming shut with a violent crack. The noise of the gate was lost in the howling wind.

At the back of the house, the gale plucked at clothes left on the line. A burst of wind yanked Josh's Little League uniform into the air, scattering clothespins. The uniform spun in the air and was swept up over the house, then tumbled through the Kopeche yard.

A branch from the oak, cracked by a bolt of lightning, hung grotesquely from the tree's trunk, flapping spasmodically, wagging above the flotsam that littered the yard.

Inside the house, Rachel woke at a crack of thunder and cried loudly, wailing with the wind, until her mother took her into the comfort of her parents' bed. Josh slept.

In the morning, the shards and shreds left by the storm were bathed in warm sunlight. The sun streamed into Josh's room, first illuminating the Mattingly poster, then highlighting two of the suspended airplanes and, finally, bathing the floor, the slot car tracks, skateboard, and the robot, which required six D batteries and had been long immobilized for lack of them.

"It's seven-thirty, Josh." Mrs. Baskin called up the stairs. "You up?"

The blankets on Josh's upper bunk shifted briefly. Then movement ceased.

The corduroy jeans Josh had worn to the carnival and his Yankee T-shirt were bunched up on the floor. The socks that had accompanied the outfit were nearer the door, not far from the right shoe. The left shoe was under the radiator.

"Sweetheart," Mrs. Baskin called again. "You'll miss the bus, and I can't drive you today!"

The blankets shifted again, this time more purposively. One at a time, two huge feet emerged from the covers and swung down over the edge of the bed. The size-twelve feet were attached to hairy ankles.

Josh did what he did every morning. Using his hands for leverage, he pushed off his upper bunk, expecting to land smoothly on the bare floor. But the floor came up too soon today. He stumbled, hitting his head on the model airplanes suspended from his ceiling. He reached for Mattingly's shoulder to stay his fall. His hand slammed against the bedroom door, smacking Mattingly sharply on the top of his batting helmet. Josh rubbed his hand idly, deciding to practice the maneuver again soon—or else abandon it.

Slowly, drowsily, Josh padded down the dim hallway to the bathroom. While he rubbed his eyes with one hand, he reached for the bathroom doorknob with the other. He only succeeded in knocking his knuckles against the wooden panel, but the door swung open. Josh reached for the light switch to the left of the door. His hand only felt bare wall. He patted the wall, first to the right, then to the left, then up, and, finally, down.

Sixteen inches down.

He shrugged and flipped the switch. Finally, the room was bathed in fluorescent light.

Josh shuffled to the bathroom mirror over the sink and opened his eyes to find himself looking straight into the light fixture atop the mirror. He glanced down at the mirror itself. There, he saw the large and mature torso of somebody else. He lowered himself until his face was eye level with the mirror, but the surprised face that met his glare was not his.

For there, in the mirror, he saw a man, not a boy. A man as old as his own father, with curly brown hair, blue eyes, and an oval face and a rather familiar nose, sort of like his mother's.

Josh spun around to see the stranger standing behind him, casting this reflection in the mirror, but he was alone. He turned back to the mirror and glared again. His eyes met with those of the image. He winked. The reflection did the same. He wrinkled his nose at the same time the man in the mirror did. He rubbed his hand on his cheek. So did the reflection, and the unfamiliar feel of stubble told him he needed a shave just as badly as the reflection did.

"No . . ." he whispered, gaping at the image in the mirror with mounting horror. "How . . ."

"Honey." Mrs. Baskin's familiar voice penetrated his pantomime from just outside the door.

Josh leapt back away from the mirror, stumbling into the shower curtain, which was suddenly all too close to the sink.

". . . I put some clean clothes out for you. Bring down your cords for the laundry, okay?"

"Okay," Josh said in an unfamiliar bass voice. He clamped his hand over his mouth in surprise.

"Are you getting a cold?" his mother asked with concern.

Josh squeezed his vocal cords tightly. "Oh, no, I'm fine," he assured her in a newfound falsetto voice. After a few seconds he heard his mother's footsteps recede down the hallway and then down the stairs to the kitchen.

When he was sure the coast was clear, Josh darted back out of the bathroom and ran down the hall to the safety of his own bedroom. He slammed the door behind him and leaned up against Don Mattingly as if to shut out the rest of the world forever.

Frantic, and unsure of what to do, he grabbed his dirty cords and began shuffling through the pockets. He found the sticky napkin from a candy apple. Stuck to one end of it was a familiar manila-colored card.

Josh held it out in front of his eyes. YOUR WISH IS GRANTED, it said.

"Omigod," Josh intoned in his new *basso vocce*, surprising himself again.

Josh's eyes darted around the room, seeking help. There was none at hand. He grabbed the clothes his mother had laid out for him so carefully, shook out the trousers and inserted first one foot and then the other. Leaning over to pull them up, he held the waistband and yanked. The trousers went only up to his knees. Josh was suddenly stuck in a pair of mini-jeans. He fell over backward and struggled desperately to remove the clothes, which had fit him until now. He yanked at the ankle.

"Breakfast is ready," his mother sang up from the kitchen.

"Be right there," he squeaked back.

Once he'd finally freed himself from the jeans, Josh swathed himself in one of his *Return of the Jedi* sheets and tiptoed toward his parents' bedroom. Josh could hear his father in the bathroom, so as long as his mother stayed in the kitchen, he'd be safe.

He opened the door. Rachel was standing in her crib, chattering happily and once again brandishing her teething ring. When Josh entered, she stared at his strange face and then burst into hysterical screams.

"Shush—shhhhhh," he said to no avail.

He grabbed her teething ring and tossed it on the rumpled bed. She was instantly silenced.

"Bring Rachel when you come down, please, Josh," Mrs. Baskin yelled up at him. He gave his sister a withering look. She returned it.

Josh riffled through his father's dresser drawers. He found a set of underwear he could fit into and some brown slacks his father wore on weekends, so he would not miss them today. From among the shirts, Josh selected a New York Giants T-shirt. His father didn't have what would have been Josh's first choice: a Yankees shirt. He grabbed some red socks from a drawer and an expensive pair of running shoes from the closet floor to complete his outfit. Satisfied, he gave Rachel back her teething ring and escaped back down the hall to his own room.

A few moments later, Josh re-emerged. The brown pants hung loosely on his hips, threatening to slide down. He snuck back to his father's closet to borrow a belt. Unable to find one, he grabbed a necktie from the rack in the closet and threaded it through the loops. The shirttails of the T-shirt covered most of the tie.

Thus attired, he lifted Rachel from her crib to take her down to the kitchen—and his mother.

While his mother was turned to the stove, Josh slid Rachel into her walker, grabbed one of his father's jackets from the coat closet, and slipped out the back door.

"Honey, you want orange juice or—" The door slammed, interrupting Mrs. Baskin. She dashed over to the door. Rachel followed her, waddling across the kitchen in her walker.

"What about your breakfast?" Mrs. Baskin called after Josh, but there was no sign of him.

Hiking up the baggy pants, Josh swung his right leg over the seat of his Stingray bicycle and sat down, pushing off down the driveway the same way he'd done thousands of times before. But his new size made it an adventure. With his feet on the pedals, Josh's knees knocked into his elbows. He lifted his elbows up away from his knees. It was hard to steer. He lowered them again; it was impossible to pedal. The elbows went up again. He reached the end of the driveway and turned right. There was no time to waste.

By the time Josh had passed the Kopeches' house, he was moving too quickly to notice that the debris from last night's storm was almost completely isolated to his own yard. He didn't even see his Little League uniform waving from the Kopeches' roof antenna. Beyond the boundary of the Baskin yard, the New Jersey town was normal. Josh noticed this because it was in sharp contrast to the way he felt. Nothing about himself, from his deep voice to his newly acquired sixteen inches, was at all normal. But soon he would be normal. As soon as he got back to the carnival, back to Zoltar.

Josh spun around the traffic circle in the middle of town, ignoring the stares of people who reacted as if they had never seen a grown man on a boy's bicycle before. He turned right at the fire station and coasted down the familiar hill, past the elementary school, toward the meadow where the carnival—

Josh squeezed the hand brakes with such unaccustomed strength that the wheels locked, shrieking in protest. He skidded to a halt. There, in front of him, was . . . nothing. There was no carnival anymore, no Avenger, no Ferris wheel, no midway, but most of all, there was no Zoltar. A lone popcorn box fluttering in the gentle breeze that rose off the river was the only remaining sign that the carnival had ever been there at all. In panic, Josh turned his bicycle around and retraced his route.

Mrs. Baskin put Rachel into her playpen in the corner of the living room and took out the upright vacuum. She plugged it in and began to work. Rachel played contentedly, pushing her toy lawn mower back and forth in the playpen. Mrs. Baskin sang to herself while she vacuumed, humming the tune from the calliope on the merry-go-round at the carnival. The front door slammed.

Mrs. Baskin looked up. There, tracking dirt across her living room, was a strange man, wearing baggy pants, a Giants T-shirt, a familiar windbreaker, and needing a shave. He had a strange look on his face—surprise, perhaps, or entreaty.

"Don't. . . . Please . . ." she uttered, backing toward the playpen to protect Rachel.

The stranger glanced at the tracks he'd left on the carpet. "Oh, I'm sorry," he said.

Shielding Rachel, Mrs. Baskin pointed at the table next to the door where her purse stood. "Take my wallet," she begged the stranger. "You can have it all."

"Mom, it's me," the stranger told her.

She'd read about psychopaths, irrational people who might harm others just for fun. Could it be that this was such a man? Surely, the strange look on his face could only mean evil.

"Don't hurt us," she pleaded.

"It's *me—Josh!*" he said.

How could this psychopath know about Josh? she asked herself. Snatching Rachel out of her playpen, Mrs. Baskin began backing into the kitchen.

The phone was in the kitchen.

"I've turned into a grownup," the man said.

She inched back along the kitchen counter.

He stepped toward her. "See, I made this wish on a machine . . ." he began.

Ignoring his delusive chatter, she passed the sink. The phone was so far away. She reached behind her, feeling along the counter edge.

"Look," the man started again. "My birthday's November third. I broke my arm when I was nine. Remember? And . . ." He paused, looking around. "Oh yeah! I'm allergic to flowers. See?" He picked up a vase filled with fresh-cut flowers and held it up to his nose. He inhaled deeply. Nothing happened.

Mrs. Baskin felt the handle of her knife drawer behind her back. Shifting Rachel to her other arm, she waited for her chance.

"Okay"—the man shrugged—"so I outgrew it; but I'm telling you, it's me," he rattled on irrationally. "My Little League team is called The Dukes. I just got a B on my history test. There's a birthmark on the back of my left knee."

Only someone who had spent time forcing information out of Josh could have learned those things— only somebody torturing him, ripping his clothes to find the birthmark. . . .

"You bastard," she hissed breathlessly in realization. "What have you done to my son?"

"I *am* your son," he countered.

Warily keeping her face to the man, she slid open the drawer and reached in, relieved to feel the firm wood handle and heft of German steel of her butcher knife. She plopped Rachel unceremoniously into the sink, produced the knife from the drawer, and brandished it at the intruder.

"Where is Josh?" she demanded, menacing him.

"Let me talk to Dad, okay?" the stranger asked.

"*Where is my child!*" Mrs. Baskin wailed at the top of her voice. With the butcher knife, she lunged wildly at the stranger.

Josh stepped backward, narrowly evading her thrust. He whirled around and fled out the kitchen door, dashing across the yard as fast as he could go.

"Police!" Mrs. Baskin shrieked, letting the knife clatter to the floor.

The word echoed through the alley, following Josh as he escaped from his home.

CHAPTER 4

BILLY Kopeche jerked his head to his right as a bulbous red ball sailed past. "Hey," he protested, his glance quickly, warily regarding the circle of his eighth-grade classmates, arrayed around him, brandishing their round red rubber weapons, "you ain't supposed to throw at the head." Billy dove and rolled as one of his grinning classmates glanced over his shoulder to see where the coach was, then hurled another shot at his head in response. "Nice shot, lame-o" he taunted, jumping to his feet and dancing like a prizefighter, whirling like a dancer.

As Billy leapt to avoid a low shot aimed at his shins, a loud *pssst* came from the partially open storeroom door in the wall beyond the circle's edge.

The whisper seemed intended to get his attention.

Billy paused, momentarily distracted. A volley of red balls was immediately launched at him from all points around the circle. Most of them hit him. He staggered and stumbled, clutched his chest convulsively, fell to the floor, twitched, closed his eyes, and *died*, all to the laughing approbation of his classmates. The bell rang.

Billy scrambled up, but his classmates had a good head start on escaping through the exits.

"Walk—don't run," the gym teacher's bass voice boomed out. "Ball monitors, put *everything* away this time."

Resolutely, Billy gathered up an armload of red balls and headed for the slightly open storeroom door. He elbowed his way in. As he was about to deposit the balls in a wire basket, the door slammed shut behind him.

He turned to stare into the desperate eyes in the unshaven face of an apparent madman in a Giants T-shirt, baggy trousers held in place with a silk tie.

"Billy, it's *me* . . . Josh," the man claimed urgently. Billy shuffled warily backward, then turned and ran for the staircase across the storeroom. "Your best friend," the stranger wailed loudly, following him.

Billy spun and heaved red balls at the man. "Yeah, and I suppose Josh was secretly the Hulk," he yelled, running up the stairs as the gym balls caromed around the room. "What have you done to my friend?" he demanded from the landing at the top of the stairs, his hand on the knob of the door.

The stranger stopped at the foot of the stairs.

> "The space goes down down down baby.
> Down down the roller coaster,"

he rapped. Billy froze, regarded the chanter and the chant intently. The man slowly edged up the stairs toward him.

> "Sweet sweet baby,
> Sweet sweet don't let me go,"

he intoned, now swaying to the cadence of the rap. He then launched into the rest of the song.

> "Shimmy shimmy ko-ko bop
> Shimmy shimmy rock
> Shimmy shimmy ko-ko bop
> Shimmy shimmy rock.
> I met a girlfriend, her name is Trisket
> She said a Trisket's really a biscuit.
> Ice cream soda pop, vanilla on the top.
> Oooo sha-li-da
> Walking down the street.
> Ten times a week.
> I met it, I said it,
> I stole my mama's credit.
> I'm cool, I'm hot,
> Sock you in the stomach three more times."

The man stopped, out of breath, a few steps below Billy.

Billy squinted his eyes, cocked his head, and stared at him. "Josh?" he said in a shocked whisper. "Can this possibly be you?" he said in awe.

"Yes," Josh said wearily, his deep voice still sounding as strange to him as it did to his friend. He lowered himself to a stair, turned to look up over his shoulder at Billy. "See, they threw me off the Avenger before I got this card from Zoltar, and then this morning my mom came after me with a butcher knife. . . ." He stopped. Billy was circling around him like a man with a Minicam filming him from every angle. He stopped, plunked down next to Josh on the stair. "What on earth am I going to do?" Josh asked.

"You look absolutely terrible," Billy told him.

That afternoon Billy retrieved a battered suitcase from the Kopeche attic, filled it with old clothing that he guessed would fit the transformed Josh, and snuck it out of the house. A police cruiser was still parked in front of the Baskin house as Billy emerged. A small knot of curious neighbors was gathered on the lawn. No one noticed Billy as he hurried off in the opposite direction for his rendezvous with Josh near the meadow where the carnival had been.

Before he had left Josh in the storeroom, even though it had made him very late for his next class, Billy had gotten his dejected friend to describe rationally the events at the carnival leading to his transformation, and to explain why his mother had tried to kill him that morning. He reviewed the information Josh had given him as he trudged thoughtfully toward their meeting.

A few minutes after his escape with Josh's CARE package, Billy lugged the suitcase into the mouth of an abandoned tunnel near the river. It was dusk. A tugboat moaned a complaint as a sight-seeing ship overtook it, heading down the Hudson. Billy deposited his burden, sat down on it, and sighed. Josh sat hud-

35

dled against the damp cement wall of the tunnel, miserably regarding his friend without greeting. Billy decided to cheer him up.

"You couldn't have maybe wished for, like, a million dollars?" he asked brightly. Josh looked at him soberly. He threw a pebble into the echoing darkness beyond the mouth of the tunnel. Billy shrugged. He squatted before the suitcase, opened it, and extracted an old leather flight jacket and battered felt hat. He rose, walked over to Josh, and dropped the hat and coat into his friend's lap.

"Don't worry, kid," Billy rasped in his best gravelly voice, squatting to level his face with Josh's. "I've got this whole thing all figured out. We get you into the City, see. . . ." He walked over to the suitcase, snapped it shut, and continued his bad Edward G. Robinson gangster imitation. ". . . And you lay low. . . ." He smoothed the air before him with a downturned palm. ". . . For a couple of days until this whole thing blows over. . . ."

Josh shrugged into the leather jacket and jammed the floppy hat onto his head. He leaned back against the wall, crossing his ankles, and spat. He then glared at Billy, daring him to continue.

"Okay," Billy went on in his own voice. "What we've got to do is find this Zoltar thing. You make a wish and, *presto*, by Thursday you're back to normal doing my homework."

"Why can't I just explain what happened and go home now?" Josh protested miserably, but at least, Billy thought, showing the first signs of life since he'd arrived. Josh continued. "I don't want to *lay low* in New York and skulk around like a bum."

"You already *tried* explaining," Billy reminded him, "and look where it got you. You want your mom trying to kill you *again*?"

"I'm going to get in a *lot* of trouble for this," Josh predicted direly, nodding for emphasis.

"No, you won't. Your folks will be so happy to see you when you get back to normal, you'll probably get a new bike and a mess of software out of it." He grabbed the suitcase. "C'mon, we gotta get going so I have time to get back before they think I've been kidnapped, too."

Josh rose and dully followed Billy out of the tunnel.

Josh took the suitcase from Billy and hefted it easily as the friends walked, in the gathering darkness, to a nearby bus stop. They sat on a bench beneath a flickering streetlight, waiting. "I'm not allowed to go into New York without . . ." Josh began, then stopped abruptly, realizing that now that he was big, he could go anywhere he wanted. Big, he thought. ". . . My folks," he finished.

Billy produced a wad of cash from the pocket of his jeans. "Here," he said, holding out the money to Josh.

Josh took the cash in his hand and asked in awe, "Where did you get this?"

"My father's top drawer."

"You *stole* it?"

"It's his emergency fund," Billy said simply. "This is an emergency."

A green and orange intercity bus labored to a stop before them, air brakes sighing. Josh and Billy stood, looked at each other intently, then climbed aboard. The doors made a hissing noise, then clunked shut behind them. Headlights probed into the blackness before them as the bus accelerated away from the stop.

CHAPTER 5

BILLY and Josh stood next to each other at the front of the crowded bus. Through the windshield, Billy watched the Manhattan skyline growing steadily larger as they sped down the highway toward the Lincoln Tunnel. "Hey, look, Josh," he said, pointing. "They've lit the top of the Empire State Building with orange lights for the fall."

Billy turned to see his friend's reaction and found himself looking directly at the word *GIANT* on Josh's chest at the level where his head *should* have been. He raised his eyes to Josh's mesmerized expression. Josh was staring blankly at his own hand, wrapped around one of the luggage rack brackets at a level he could not have even reached the day before. Billy tugged at Josh's leather sleeve.

"I said, they've made the Empire State Building orange for the fall," he said, pointing.

Josh bent over at the waist so that he could see out the front window, too. "Yeah, they have," he said, straightened, and resumed staring at his hand.

A few minutes later Billy emerged from the Port Authority Terminal with Josh, suitcase in hand, trailing behind and gawking at his surroundings. They crossed Eighth Avenue and walked eastward on Forty-second Street, in the direction of Times Square.

The street was brightly lit by theatre marquees—just as it had been on the occasional afternoons when the friends had snuck into town, against parental prohibitions, to sample the video game parlors and fast-food emporiums that punctuated the Times Square area.

"How many X's do you suppose a movie can get?" Josh interrupted Billy's reverie to ask.

"Looks to me like most of them get three," Billy responded. "Wanna get some Arkansas, Kansas, Louisiana, or Tennessee fried chicken?"

"How about an adult book from one of these stores with the windows painted over?" Josh asked.

Billy paused, considering. "Nah," he said.

They walked uptown on Seventh Avenue and turned the corner onto Forty-fifth Street. A tall, slim woman in a very short red dress with a shawl slung negligently over her back and arms detached herself from the side of a building and, ignoring Billy, sashayed over to Josh.

"You wanna ditch the kid and have a date, big

fella?'' she asked Josh from behind a mask of makeup and mascara.

"Naw, I hate dates," Josh said brightly. "Prunes, too. You got any apples?"

"Jo-osh . . ." Billy began.

The woman stepped between Josh and Billy. She was standing very close to Josh, her hand on his arm, gazing up into his eyes boldly, thrusting her chest out at him. Josh looked down.

Very little material had been involved in the making of the top part of her tight dress.

"A smart guy, huh," she purred. "I *like* smart guys," she announced, glancing around as if to find anyone who would disagree with her about her preference. She noticed Billy. He noticed her back.

"Why don't you send junior here"—she bobbed her head toward Billy— "home, so we can party?"

"Party," Josh repeated, mystified.

"Yeah, party." She leered at him. "You know, you look like just the kind of man who might really enjoy going around the world with me."

"Gee, I dunno." Josh was puzzled. "So far, I've never been any further away than Pennsylvania."

"Josh Baskin," Billy said sharply. "This woman is *not* a travel agent. She's a hooker." The woman glared at him. "A bim," he taunted her. "Whore, prostitute, streetwalker, *puta*."

Josh regarded his friend and the party girl with skepticism. "You gotta be kiddin' me," he announced to them intently. Then he tore off his hat, threw it to the sidewalk, and laughed uproariously at the notion that such a preposterous thing could actually be hap-

41

pening to him in real life. "You *must* be kiddin' me,"
he managed to repeat incredulously through his con-
tinuing laughter.

The woman glanced back and forth between the
youngster and the grownup, puzzling over which was
which. Another pair of lunatics, she concluded. She
spun on her spiked heel and strode rapidly down the
street.

H-O-T-E-L . . . H-O-T-E-L . . . The pink neon
light blinked in the middle of the block on Forty-fifth.

"Come on, Josh," Billy said. "There's a place you
can stay."

Josh picked up his suitcases and followed Billy down
the block. The street was dark. Most of the lights were
broken. The doorways served as shelters and, in some
cases, headquarters for local businesses. Overdressed,
underclothed women loitered under the few unbroken
streetlights, displaying their wares. Josh and Billy
scurried down the block to the hotel.

Billy looked up at the doors, filthy and forbidding.

"This seems okay," he said hopefully.

"No, it doesn't," Josh told him.

Undaunted and searching for signs of encourage-
ment, Billy spotted the hotel's name on a sign of peeling paint bolted to the masonry. "*St. James*, Josh,"
he said. "It's *religious*."

Josh looked at Billy for a moment, considering
whether his friend had actually lost his mind.

"Come on, Josh," Billy said.

Josh followed him reluctantly up the steps.

The inside of the St. James fulfilled its outside

promise. It was dark and dingy. The lobby was filthy, disgusting, and dilapidated. But it smelled bad.

A thick Plexiglas partition separated them from the room clerk. He was barely visible behind a sign that read FIREARMS KEPT ON PREMISES. Josh approached him timidly.

"Uh . . . we need a room," he explained.

The clerk eyed the pair suspiciously. "Seventeen-fifty a night," he said. "Ten-dollar deposit on the sheets. In advance."

Josh drew the cash Billy had given him from his jacket pocket. Glancing nervously at his surroundings, he hurriedly peeled off twenty-seven dollars and returned the rest of the bills to his pocket. He fished two quarters from his trouser pocket and slapped them on top of the bills on the counter. He slid the payment across the counter and through a narrow slit in the partition.

"Third floor," the man said, shoving a key back at Josh.

The pair trailed down the grim hallway of the third floor, passing graffiti consisting primarily of phone numbers and consumer reports. With every step, Josh became more worried. With every step, Billy became more determinedly optimistic. A pair of derelicts camped on the doorstep of one of the rooms. Embarrassed, Josh glared at the opposite wall.

"This is my friend. He's moving in," Billy announced cheerfully.

The derelicts didn't react to either of them.

The door to Josh's room swung open without the

use of the key, because the lock was broken. Josh's heart sank. The small, square room was lit by a single bulb suspended from the ceiling. A dented iron bedstead was burdened only with a stained two-inch-thick mattress that sagged nonetheless. The chipped and peeling bureau looked like a Salvation Army reject, and the lone chair retained only two of its original four back slats. The seat was covered by a square of plywood. A stained sink protruded from the wall in one corner. Brownish water dripped from the cold faucet.

"I'm not gonna do it," Josh said. "I'm not gonna stay here!"

Billy backed toward the door. "You'll be fine," he said confidently. "You go to sleep now. You wake up, you won't even know I was gone."

Realization hit Josh. "You never said you were going to leave!" he wailed.

"I can't help it, Josh," Billy reasoned. "I'm supposed to be home by ten."

Josh gaped at his friend. Home! What a wonderful word. What a wonderful place. His own things, his own bed, his own family—even Rachel. "I'm going with you," Josh said, bolting for the door.

Billy grasped him by the tie that was serving as a belt and dragged his friend back across the room to the decrepit bed. "Look," he reasoned, "if I don't come home tonight, there's going to be two kids missing. You want the cops out looking for *both* of us?" Josh stopped resisting. Billy released him. "I'll cut school tomorrow and we'll find that Zoltar machine before you know it, okay?"

Josh paused a moment, then exhaled deeply.

"Just one night." Billy said. "All right?"

Josh glanced around his new home and shivered. "All right. Just one, huh?"

"Right," Billy assured him. He stood up from the bed and walked toward the door.

"What if I can't sleep?" Josh asked.

Billy turned back and looked at him. Then he appraised the room gravely. "It's probably better if you don't" he advised his friend. "I'll see you in the morning," he said, reaching gingerly for the door-knob.

"What time?" Josh asked, delaying Billy's departure again.

"Eight-thirty," Billy said. He stepped across the sill and glanced down the hallway. He was leaving. Josh knew it. Billy paused a second before walking away. He turned back, smiling "Oh, and, uh, I'd use the chain lock on the door if I were you," he advised. The door closed. Billy's familiar footsteps echoed down the bare hall and then were gone.

Josh stood uneasily in the center of his room. The filthy institutional-green walls were stained from years of neglect. The yellowed linoleum floor hadn't seen the business end of a mop in a generation. A battered television was chained and bolted to the floor. This offered no solace. Josh stepped over to the window, darkened with a greasy roll-up shade. He tugged at the bottom. The roll sprang free of the bracket and came crashing down onto the cold radiator. Josh jumped back in surprise.

H-O-T-E-L . . . H-O-T-E-L . . . blinked in his face, lighting up the room with its eerie pink glow.

Through the open window, a siren wailed, joined by a second siren in the distance. A nearby car backfired—or *was* it a backfire? Josh slammed the window closed.

He turned to the bureau, whose last coat of paint, probably Depression era, Josh thought, had been an ill-advised orange. Josh shuddered. He took the set of yellowed sheets from the dresser and stepped over to the bare-mattressed bed. He unfurled a sheet to make the bed and tried to ignore the groan of bedsprings from next door. A telephone rang so loudly that Josh jumped again.

There was no phone in his room, but the ringing was insistent. He froze.

He recalled a pay phone in the hall immediately outside his door. Then he heard the thunder of footsteps outside. The ringing stopped.

"*Qué?*" a loud voice demanded unpleasantly.

Josh sprang to the door, which quaked loosely in its jamb. He slammed his body against it, to ward off invaders. His own hand shook while he slid the chain lock into its track and drove the bolt home.

"*Te odio!*" the man cursed into the telephone inches away. Josh fled from the doorway. The walls, door, and window of this place were no protection from the world outside. Josh was exposed to all its very adult evils.

Then the phone conversation suddenly took on a new burst of spiteful energy. Josh could only imagine what was being said, but at the crescendo, the man screamed into the phone and slammed the receiver down. The wall shivered. Paint rattled to the floor.

46

Josh dived onto his nearly made bed, clutching the bare pillow for solace it could not give him. He trembled helplessly. A lone tear ran down his cheek.

He was a boy in a man's body—trapped in no man's land.

CHAPTER 6

THE next morning, Billy and Josh burst through the front door of the dingy St. James Hotel and dashed down the steps into the bright sunlight that bathed the tawdry neighborhood.

Billy had arrived early with a plan—and a bag containing a razor and accessories. Now a Band-Aid decorated Josh's right cheek. He held a spotted tissue to his chin. "Ouch! That stings," he complained, gingerly touching the scrape on his cheek. A small red circle on the tissue enlarged. "Think it'll ever stop bleeding?" he asked Billy.

"Of course it will," Billy assured him.

"Am I going to have to do this every day?"

"If you mean *shave*, yes. If you mean lacerate yourself, I hope not. You're going to need transfusions if you lose that much blood every day.''

"I never thought it would be like this,'' Josh said. "It always looks so easy when Dad does it. Maybe I'll grow a beard.''

"Give me a break,'' Billy said, then he changed the subject. "Look, I've been thinking about your problem—''

"The bleeding?''

"No, Zoltar, Josh. The way I see it, somebody's gotta have a record of these things. So, the first thing we do is to get a list of carnivals within, say, a fifty-mile radius, and then we begin the hunt. Here, take this.'' He handed Josh a token that he had fished out of his pocket.

"I don't need this,'' Josh said, giving it back to Billy. "I always just wait until the clerk isn't looking and scoot under the turnstile.''

"Not anymore, you don't, mister,'' Billy informed him, returning the token.

"What do you want?'' the clerk at the administration building information desk asked, as if their presence were a personal nuisance to her.

"A list of carnivals within fifty miles of the city,'' Billy said.

"And fairs,'' Josh added.

"*And* arcades,'' Billy finished.

The line at the information booth snaked behind them, curving tentatively toward the door through which they'd walked hours before. The price of information in this place was time—and the clerk had all of it in the world.

Slowly, she turned to locate the six-inch-thick book behind her. Slowly, she hefted it. Slowly, she turned toward the inquirers again. Slowly, she opened the volume.

"Carnivals," she intoned.

"And fairs."

"And arcades," Billy and Josh reminded her.

Slowly, she turned the pages.

"Try Consumer Affairs, third floor, room 3211," she suggested. Slowly, she turned to replace the book she'd need again for her very next customer.

They fled.

After another interminable wait, they reached the information window at Consumer Affairs. Billy explained what they needed and waited expectantly. In answer, the gray-haired woman shoved a form at him.

"Fill this out in triplicate," she said. "Five-dollar filing charge."

They *had* come to the right place. Their problems were nearly solved. "Terrific!" Billy said excitedly, reaching for the ball-point pen at the woman's elbow, only to find it was attached by a beaded chain without enough beads to reach anyplace useful.

"One month to process," the woman said, as if there had been no interruption. "You'll get it in six weeks."

"Six weeks!" Josh howled.

The woman shrugged. "Sometimes longer, but you could get lucky," she said doubtfully.

The remaining blood drained from Josh's face.

* * *

"I'm going to be thirty years old for the rest of my life," Josh complained as he ambled listlessly along the sidewalk behind Billy. The two had finished the paperwork in the administration building, and now both were facing the fact that there was nothing to do but to wait. Six weeks.

"Aw, come on," Billy said as cheerfully as he could. "We'll figure something out." He grabbed the pole of a No Parking sign and spun around it. Josh did the same. "By the way, you're closer to thirty-five," Billy informed Josh.

Josh kicked at a trash can. The lid was fastened to the can's handle by a chain. It was totally useless as a shield.

"I'll come every day after school," Billy promised.

"How?" Josh challenged him.

Billy put one foot on the top of a fire hydrant and sprang upward, landing softly on the other side. Josh did the same. It was easier for him now that he was six feet tall.

"I'll tell them I'm on the basketball team," Billy said.

"I'm dead," Josh announced. He sank to the sidewalk, sitting on the curb with his back against the wire mesh of a city trash can. Billy plunked down next to him.

"We're getting the list," Billy reminded him. "We've just got to hang on for a while."

"That's easy for you to say." Josh picked up an advertisement for a massage parlor and began folding it expertly into a paper airplane. "You still get lunch money. What am I going to live on?'' Josh asked. He lofted the airplane across the street. It hit a lady who was clutching her small daughter's hand tightly as she hustled along. She paused to give Billy a frown, then hurried on.

Billy shrugged, as if the question of money were an easy one. "So, you'll get a job," he said simply.

"A *what?*" Josh asked, as if he'd never heard the word before. He stared at Billy.

"You're a grownup now," Billy said. "You're allowed to get a job. In fact, most grownups have them. Even my mom. *Especially* my mom."

"I can't get a job," Josh protested.

"Sure you can," Billy said. "It can't be any tougher than school. We'll just find something you're good at."

Josh gave him a withering look.

"There's got to be something here," Billy said, his eyes on the newspaper opened in front of him. The pair sat in the booth of an ice cream store, devouring the banana split between them on the counter. Josh was working from the marshmallow end, Billy the pineapple end. By agreement, they would meet at strawberry by way of hot fudge.

"Cardiological technician . . . Civil engineer," Billy recited, stumbling slightly on *cardiological*. "I think that has to do with hearts. It's serious."

"You want your cherry?" Josh asked.

"Go ahead," Billy said affably. "I'll take some of your chopped walnuts. Clerical transcriber. Can you do that?"

"Hey, Billy?" Josh asked, interrupting his friend.

"Yeah?" Billy asked, looking up reluctantly.

Josh opened his mouth to reveal a glob of melted hot fudge and ice cream with masticated cherry on top. He waggled his tongue for effect.

"Gross!" Billy said in frank admiration.

"Go to the other column," Josh told him, tapping the newspaper.

"Oh, yeah," Billy said. "Okay, collection agent? Company clerk—who knows what that means? Computer operator . . . Construction . . ."

"Hey, I can do that," Josh said.

"What, construction?"

"No, computer operator. I'm good at that. I've just about got the Ice Wizard licked, you know—"

Billy gazed at his friend and then looked back down at the advertisement. "MacMillan Toys," he read. "Toys!"

"Billy," Josh said. "I think we're onto something. What else does it say?"

"Experienced computer operators. Must perform data updates, malfunction isolation, monitoring of cluster performance—"

"I can do all that stuff," Josh said.

"You can? That's not Ice Wizards, you know," Billy said.

"I know, but it's the same thing in theory. I've done all those things on my computer. The only difference between mine and theirs is probably a gigabyte or two. Let me see." He took the paper from Billy and read on. "Hey, great, they use HP 3000's."

"You understand that?" Billy asked.

"Well, it's an old system, but—"

"Where do we go?" Billy, the Man of Action, asked.

Josh finished reading the ad. "Apply in person: MacMillan Toys."

"Let's go!" Billy said with newfound enthusiasm.

CHAPTER 7

HALF an hour later, Billy and Josh busied themselves filling out their second endless form of the day. Josh had removed his Band-Aid and the pieces of tissue that had staunched the flow of blood earlier. Only a few small dark red scabs remained as a painful reminder of the trials of adulthood.

The job application form was more complicated than the form at the Consumer Affairs department had been. Josh could manage the questions about name and address, but after that, he was stuck.

"Previous employment?" he hissed at Billy. The fifteen other people in the room filling out the same form stared at him.

"Your paper route," Billy reminded him.

Josh nodded, relieved. "Right," he said, and began scratching at the form once again.

"SSAN? What's that?" he asked.

"Social Security Account Number," Billy translated.

Josh was stumped. Once more, Billy came to the rescue.

"Thirty-five, seventeen, twenty-three, fourteen, nine."

"What's that?" Josh asked, scribbling down the numbers.

"My locker combination," Billy said.

"Your locker ends in a four," Josh retorted.

"But that's too many numbers, ding-o" Billy said.

"Mr. Baskin?" a singsong feminine voice called.

Startled to hear his father's name, Josh sat up and looked around. His eyes lit on the receptionist who had spoken. She wasn't calling his father at all. She was calling *him*. He stood, knees feeling more like spaghetti than bone.

"Yes?" he answered.

"The personnel director, David Halloran, will see you now," she informed him.

"Oh, thanks," he said, suddenly embarrassed. He wasn't used to grownups addressing him so politely. The clipboard with his application attached was clutched tightly in his sweaty hand. Billy stood next to him.

"Your son can wait for you out here," the receptionist said sweetly. "We'll take care of him—see that he doesn't get into any trouble."

Billy stopped, a frozen smile on his face. Josh turned

to him. "Sport, you sit right over there and don't be a nuisance," he intoned.

"Sure, *Dad*," Billy sputtered, his face quickly turning to crimson as he stifled a laugh. At just the critical moment, he coughed, instead. Josh coughed, too, then followed the receptionist out of the room, mumbling something about how hard it was to get rid of flu at this time of year. The receptionist didn't seem to care.

A job interview, Josh found, was very much like spending time in the vice principal's office. The person on the other side of the desk asked questions, and Josh tried to evade them cleverly enough so he wouldn't get tripped up.

The personnel director even looked like the George Washington Junior High School vice principal. He was in his forties, balding, and wore an ever so slightly frayed blue suit. His necktie was locked in place with a tie clip that was too big, its fake gold flaking.

"So," he said. "Says here you've got four years of experience on the *Jersey Journal*."

"Yeah, four years," Josh confirmed nervously. "That's right."

"All on computers?"

"Yes, sir," Josh said. After all, he told himself, he'd done all his customers' bills on his computer.

"I'm having a bit of trouble with your handwriting, Mr. Baskin. Where did you go to school?"

"George Washington, sir," Josh answered honestly.

"Oh, G.W. !" Mr. Halloran responded enthusiastically. "My brother-in-law got his doctorate there. Fine school. Really fine school," he said proudly.

Suddenly, there was a bond between the two of them. Josh didn't know how it had been forged, but he was relieved that it was. He smiled and nodded in response.

"Did you pledge?" the man asked.

Still nodding, Josh answered him. "Every morning," he assured the man.

At that moment, Mr. Halloran's office door burst open. A woman stormed in, totally oblivious to Josh's presence. She was old, perhaps thirty, with light brown hair stylishly cut. She was dressed for success, in a gray pin-striped suit with a straight skirt, contrasted by a burgundy blouse and accented with a single strand of pearls. She wore matching pearl earrings. On her wrist were several gold chains—enough to provide evidence she had Arrived. Josh leaned over curiously and noticed her shapely legs, descending into conservative black leather pumps.

She noticed nothing about Josh.

"It happened again, David!" she sputtered. "That girl is absolutely useless. You've got to find me someone who knows what she's doing!" She glared at the personnel director and then, for the first time, became aware that she was actually interrupting something. "Excuse me," she said hurriedly, insincerely, and then continued. "I'm not getting any messages. Nothing's been filed. Ever since she got engaged, her work and my life have been a disaster!"

"Well, Susan," he began. "She came with the highest—"

"Do you know what she does all day?" the woman named Susan asked in total outrage. "She's spent the last three months writing down her married name. Over and over and over. Mrs. Judy Hicks. Mrs. David Hicks. Mrs. Judy Mitchelson-Hicks. Sometimes with the hyphen, sometimes without the hyphen. Sometimes she *spells* the hyphen!"

Susan had struck home with the spelled-out hyphen. "Oh," David said thoughtfully. "Well, I don't know where we could put her—"

"I do," Susan said. "Put her on unemployment!" With that, she turned on her voguish heels and strode out, slamming the door behind her. David stared after her for a while, then, still flustered, returned his attention to Josh.

"Well, all of this looks in order," he said, trying to smooth over the abrupt interruption. "How soon can you start?" he asked.

Josh decided, right then and there, that being a grownup was a breeze.

Outside the door of the personnel department, Susan Lawrence paused momentarily to compose herself after her outburst at Halloran. It was good, she thought, to put staff employees in their place, to let them know that line people, the ones who made the cash register ring, were the people who *really* mattered in the firm.

It was not bad manners to yell at a troll, she reasoned as she now strolled to the elevator that would lift her back to the executive suite. You had to be rude just to get their attention. She stabbed the elevator button with a crimson-tipped finger, turning her wrist thoughtfully as she did so.

As she left the elevator at the executive floor, Susan smiled smugly. It was always a pleasure to be back where she belonged, her heels sinking deep into the plush carpeting, the rich wood paneling and expensive oil paintings of the marketing department rewarding the senses for what intellect and moxie accomplished for the firm.

And it was a particular relief to escape the gray steel desks and cheap prints and linoleum floors of one of the departments that contributed only to overhead, not to the bottom line.

As Susan rounded the corner near her office, some of the upper-echelon gilt was eroded by peals of laughter coming from the secretarial pool. The area was festooned with balloons and streamers and littered with debris of shopping bags and wrapping paper. At the center of the commotion was the incipient Mrs. Judy Mitchelson Hyphen Hicks, her desk stacked with gaily wrapped presents and opened boxes and surrounded by her alternately laughing and cheering clerical cohorts.

It was tacky.

"What's the joke?" Susan demanded of the receptionist.

The younger woman looked up, startled, from where she was scribbling a phone message. "Oh, Miss Lawrence—"

"*Ms*. Lawrence!" Susan corrected impatiently.

"Is it a small?" Judy inquired from the eye of the storm.

Her friends roared with laughter. The receptionist giggled and confided to Susan, "See, when she opens her shower presents, everything she says is what she'll say on her wedding night. Only she doesn't know it, so when we read the list to her—"

"Who's answering the phones?" Susan interrupted her.

"Oh, I . . ." She meekly handed Susan the message she had taken. Susan snatched it from her hand, stormed into her office, and slammed the door against the din outside.

Ignoring the noise of the party, which penetrated the walls despite her closed door, Susan strode to her desk and dropped into her high-backed leather executive chair.

"It's so *fuzzy*," Judy screamed from outside, only to be drowned out by another wave of laughter.

Susan leaned back in her chair, crossed her ankles on an open drawer, and reflexively tugged the hem of her skirt down primly. She pulled the receiver from the phone and punched in some numbers. "Susan Lawrence," she told the instrument casually. "Is he in?"

Susan dropped her feet to the floor, swiveled to face forward, her elbows propped on the blotter. "Paul . . ." she breathed urgently into the phone, ". . . if I don't have a man tonight . . ." she whispered, ". . . I am absolutely going to . . ." She stopped. "Yeah," she said disgustedly in an otherwise more businesslike voice, "I'll hold."

She stared vaguely into the middle distance across the top of a paperless desk. On the desk's forward edge were a small crystal vase holding two pink silk roses and a sterling gatefold framing pictures of her sisters, one of them beaming at an infant in her arms. Susan twisted the phone cord in her hand and gazed at the long golden hair of Princess Gwendoline, MacMillan's new top-of-the-line doll, in the middle of the blotter.

"Oh, it's pink," Judy's voice again pierced the walls, followed by the laughter of her audience.

Susan cocked her head to the side to hold the phone receiver and picked up Gwendoline. She pressed an invisible button in the doll's back, regrasped the phone, and leaned back. "These are the preliminary voice runs on Princess Gwendoline," an incongruously deep masculine voice emitted from a tinny speaker in the belly of the doll. "All comments should be directed to Jack Taylor no later than Thursday."

There was a faint whirring sound, then a high, squeaky voice announced, "One day I'll find my prince."

Then the man's voice, sternly, "Alternate version number one."

Then a lower, silkier feminine "One day my prince will come."

"Alternate version number two," the male voice intoned.

"I want you to steal all the money from Mommy's purse . . ." Alternate Voice One then urged conspiratorily, ". . . and buy all my accessories. The more you buy for me, the more I'll love you in return."

"Just kidding, Susan," the male voice told her.

Susan didn't find her recorded colleague funny. She grimaced.

Judy chose that moment to scream again from the deep end of the secretarial pool. "This'll *never* fit!"

CHAPTER 8

WITH the shrieking protest of steel wheels on the sharply curved steel rails of the Fourteenth Street Station still ringing in his ears, Josh emerged uncertainly from the vast labyrinth that undermines Union Square.

The grownups—the *other* grownups—hurrying to their jobs around him all seemed to know exactly how to find their way out of the underworld. *They* knew where they were going and what they were going to do. Their faces were placid, their manner purposeful but casual. The business of going to work obviously did not hold the terror for them that Josh's first day held for him.

Josh practiced looking purposeful and casual at the same time. He surged across Fourteenth Street with the crowd and swaggered north past the statue of Mahatma Gandhi and along the perimeter of the Square past the trucks and booths of the green market. Strolling casually across Seventeenth Street, he was nearly run down by a taxi careening around the corner from Broadway. The cabbie rolled down his window and screamed at Josh as he scrambled to the curb. Josh gave the driver a bird. No one paid any attention. He shrugged and continued on his way to the MacMillan Toy Building.

Josh looked up the location of the Data Processing Division on the board in the lobby, then ascended in the elevator. In Data Processing he reported to Mr. Fitzgerald, as he had been directed on the previous afternoon.

Fitzgerald's secretary told Josh where to hang his jacket and handed him an identification tag with a Polaroid picture taken the previous day. The laminated card also had his name and employee number on it. Josh glanced at the card and almost handed it back to the secretary. Then he realized that it *was* his picture and not that of some older stranger.

He winced just looking at the bold red spots of the shaving cuts on his face on the I. D. card. As Billy had predicted, this morning had gone better. Only one cut.

Fitzgerald shook his hand and escorted Josh through a set of double doors and into a large room containing a platoon of identical gray steel desks bearing identical computer terminals. Fitzgerald steered Josh to the center of the room to a desk with an overflowing in-basket and invited him to sit.

"I thought we'd start you off on last week's preschool orders," Fitzgerald said. "That should take a few days and give you some time to find your way around. Do you smoke?" he asked suspiciously.

"Well, I did one time, but—"

"Only on breaks in the coffee room," he warned. Then he waved his hand at the in basket. "Most of this is pretty straightforward stuff, but if you have any questions, come to me." He patted Josh on the shoulder. "Welcome aboard," he said. "And good luck."

Josh watched Fitzgerald's back as he retreated through the double doors.

He sat down on his chair. The casters rolled easily across the linoleum floor. He pulled himself toward his work station and, bracing against the desk, turned. The swivel seat spun to the right. He arrested the spin and pushed the other way. He found he could keep it going by hustling his feet around the splayed legs at the chair's base. It was neat. When he was dizzy, he finally stopped.

He flicked his monitor on and glanced around to see what everyone else was doing. "Morning," a voice behind him announced brightly. Josh swiveled. The sandy-haired man at the next desk smiled, rose, and extended his hand. "Scotty Brennan."

Josh stood and shook Brennan's hand. "Hi," he said, at a loss for a more cordial response.

Scotty looked at Josh's badge. "Name's Baskin, right?"

"How'd you know that?" Josh asked.

"Gotta know everything in a place like this. Get you some coffee?" he said, stepping out from behind his desk.

66

"If they don't have any Yoo Hoo," Josh replied.

Scotty turned and gave him a sharp look. "Regular, right?"

"Nah, fill it up with 97 Octane Super Premium Hi-Test," Josh told Scotty's retreating back. "You may not know, but your carburetor knows. . . ."

Josh paged through one of the printouts on his desk. A loud giggle arose from two desks over, where a woman was huddled over her phone, whispering into it. Josh studied her. Of course, the phone . . . He glanced back at his desk. They had given him a phone, too! One you didn't have to feed quarters.

He punched a number into the phone quickly, ducked into the well beneath his desk with the receiver. "Hello, Mrs. Baskin," he said softly when he heard her voice. "How are you?"

"Who is this?" his mother snapped.

"Um, I just wanted you to know that Josh is fine and that he's okay and everything like that."

"You have my boy," she accused him, her voice rising.

"Well, yes, but you're going to get him back just the way he was."

"Let me talk to Josh," she demanded with artificial calm.

"Well, he can't come to the phone right now."

"Why? What have you done to him?" Her voice rose again.

"*I* didn't do *anything* to him. I think he's an absolutely terrific kid."

"I want proof that he's all right," she said icily.

"Okay. Go ahead. Ask me something. Ask me

something that only he knows, anything at all, and I'll ask him for you. Then you'll know he's really okay. Okay? Anything. Ask.''

Josh thought that his mother had hung up, because there was a long silence. Then she said softly, ''Ask him what I used to sing to him at bedtime when he was little.''

Josh covered the mouthpiece of the telephone with his hand. ''Oh, shit,'' he said to himself. He moved his hand and cajoled, ''Isn't there something else you'd—''

''Ask him,'' she screamed.

''All right. Al-ll right.'' Josh put his hand over the phone again, cleared his throat, and hummed to remind himself of the tune. It didn't come out right. He tried again, whistling this time. Then he removed his hand and sang softly into the phone. ''Love, love me do. You know I love you. I'll always . . .'' He stopped.

His mother was crying.

''Aw, c'mon. . . . Look, you'll see him real soon. Cross my heart and hope to . . .'' A cup was set on his desk with a soft clunk. Josh emerged from under the desk. Scotty was looking at him curiously. Josh turned away, spoke into the phone brusquely. ''Look, we'll discuss this again later. Okay?''

It was hard. She was still crying.

Josh listened, then resolutely hung up.

''I know all about it,'' Scotty said.

Josh looked up at him in dismay, ''You do?''

''C'mere,'' Scotty responded crooking his finger at Josh. He rose slowly from his chair and stepped over to where Scotty was standing.

Scotty put his arm around Josh's shoulders and nodded conspiratorily down the aisle of desks. "See that one over there in the red?" he whispered avuncularly to Josh.

Josh nodded. She was built and made up like the "travel agent" he and Billy had met the other evening.

"She'll wrap her legs around you and squeeze so tight you'll be begging for mercy."

"Oh, ah, thanks," Josh responded, puzzled. "I'll try to stay away from her."

Scotty regarded Josh from under furrowed eyebrows.

Susan flattened against the corridor wall as a loose column of gawky nine-year-olds straggled past. The youngsters were led, Pied Piper–fashion, by a bespectacled dweeb from Market Research who chanted instructions to which no one paid any evident attention. "You'll be given fifteen minutes to play with each toy. At the end of that time, we will ask you a series of questions to determine your responses."

A clever hidden purpose for a series of questions, Susan thought.

"Remember, no throwing, no roughhousing or unnecessary chitchat during the test—er—play period. But you *are* to have fun." Market Research stopped, regarded his charges. "Any questions?"

"Where's the bathroom?" volunteered a high-pitched voice from the back of the line.

"We already passed it," the researcher responded impatiently, and headed around the corner with a representative fraction of his firm's target market in ragged pursuit.

Susan resumed her journey to the end of the hallway. She paused before the door there to straighten her hair and check her makeup in the shiny brass plate. The sign read:

PAUL DAVENPORT
SENIOR VICE PRESIDENT

Susan installed a smile, knocked lightly, and entered.

Paul's corner office was twice as large as Susan's. In addition to his huge desk in the corner across the room, there were acres of space for the sitting area, which Susan now crossed, and for the small conference table and wet bar in the opposite corner.

Shelves and racks along the interior wall held a child's fantasy of successes past, present, and prospective by the office's upwardly mobile occupant.

At the desk, Paul intently examined what Susan recognized as the new Mitor action figure prototype. She strode up to the desk, planted her palms on the gleaming surface, and launched.

"Trouble," she said ominously.

"We're pregnant?" he inquired mildly, raising his eyebrows—but not too much.

Paul's black hair was carefully styled to fall boyishly across the high forehead of his youthful, handsome face. He wore regulation red suspenders to pick up the polka dots of his yellow power tie. Invisible stays disciplined the collar points of his European-cut Custom

70

Shop pinpoint oxford cloth shirt. Bulbous button-downs were out. So were shirt-pocket initials. Paul's were on his sleeve. His heart, Susan felt, was not.

Susan shook her head impatiently, collapsed into one of the armchairs fronting the desk, brought her slim Mark Cross attaché case to her lap. "Huggybear took a nosedive," she told him.

Paul's smile vanished. He straightened in his chair, regarded Susan gravely.

She popped the golden clasps of the attaché and extracted a manila envelope. Rising and setting aside the case, she placed the envelope before him like a burnt offering. "Take a look at those numbers, Paul," she suggested. He slid papers out, studied them.

"Third-quarter profits are off forty percent," she continued. "Preorders are down fifty-five percent. And we're not talking about one goddamn toy." She crossed her legs for emphasis and to keep Paul's attention focused. "We're talking here about the whole goddamn line: Huggybear Papa, Huggybear Mama . . . the goddamn *Baby* is off sixty percent."

"You must feel awful," Paul finally responded, calmly.

Susan studied Paul carefully to make sure she had heard him right. "*I* must feel awful?"

"You must," he said, his rising inflection finishing near a squeak.

"Paul . . . I think . . . *we* feel awful," she reminded him evenly.

"Well, yeah." He shrugged. "The fact that you must feel bad means that I must feel bad for you, too."

Susan sorted out his construction. She didn't like it.

"Paul . . ." Her voice was rising in outrage. "This whole freakin' Huggy thing was your idea from front to back."

"I think if you just go right on in there and talk to MacMillan . . ."

"It's not *my* fault."

"Time out, Susan, honey." He showed her a pair of carefully manicured hands in a referee's T. "What are we trying to do here? Are we trying to fix this thing, or are we trying to place blame?" He rose from his chair, walked around the desk, and sat on the forward edge. He caressed the side of her face with a perfectly dry palm. "If it will make you feel better, I'll go talk to him with you myself."

The conversation with MacMillan about the Huggybear disaster flowed out of the top-floor office suite, where it had begun, and continued on the elevator. MacMillan was on his way down to a meeting with the Market Research Department.

"Bullshit, Paul," the founder and CEO announced calmly but firmly as the three executives emerged from the elevator and stopped to talk. "Let's not lie to ourselves. If the kids like a toy, it sells. Period."

Susan studied her boss—Mac, he was called—as he spoke. He looked, she thought, both distinguished and comfortable with the nickname. Mac was clad in the standard navy-blue pinstripe of the investment banker. His trim salt-and-pepper hair surrounded a craggy face with bright blue eyes that penetrated through phony arguments like Paul's expressed willingness to *take the blame* for *Susan's* mistake. . . .

The lines in Mac's face, the crinkles at the corners of the eyes, told of a man who laughed like a child, often and deeply. There was, in fact, much of the child in Mac. Maybe that was why he seemed, somehow, *internally* calm—loving to pretend, hating pretense, and able to tell the difference. Wasn't that what being a child meant? Susan wondered. Not being hurt by your own hopes, not being fooled by your own folly?

She ended her reverie as they continued down the corridor toward Research. We *should* have been able to predict that Huggybear was a bust before full-scale production, she thought. "Every bit of research and focus testing show that—" she began.

"Yes, it worked with the research," Mac interrupted. "It worked with the testing; it just didn't work with the kids."

As if on cue, Josh hurtled around the corner, carrying a huge stack of papers in his arm and looking back over his shoulder at Scotty, who was trailing behind. Josh crashed into Susan, and the papers flew into the air as he staggered backward. Susan fell into Mac, who was, in turn, bowled over by the impact. The papers fluttered to the carpet around the fallen.

"Uh, hi," Josh said, recognizing Susan as the woman from Halloran's office. "Did you get that problem with your secretary fixed?" he ended lamely.

"Why don't you watch where the hell you're going, you yotz," Paul shouted at Josh. Josh cringed. This was it for his two-day-old career.

"Oh, I'm sorry." Josh was contrite. "Are you hurt,

Mister?'' he asked. Meanwhile, Scotty was helping Susan to her feet.

Paul helped Mac.

"Are you okay?" Susan asked Mac.

"I'm fine," he responded with a smile.

Paul glared at Josh. "You could kill someone, running around here like that."

"I doubt it, Paul," Mac asserted. "I'm fine, son," he told Josh. Then, looking back at Paul intently, he told his colleague, "It's good to fall on your ass every once in a while." The he stooped and began to gather the papers that Josh had dropped.

This got Josh four extra pairs of hands to help with the work.

"Where were you going in that awful hurry, son?"

"Well, I was supposed to get these copied and the machine downstairs was broken and they needed them by five, so—"

"Good for you, son," Mac interrupted. "Keep it up," he said to Josh, patting his shoulder and rising. "Nothing wrong with it, Paul," he said, looking at him. "Nothing at all."

Mac moved off for his meeting. Paul threw down the papers he had retrieved and stomped off. Looking at Josh strangely, Susan handed him her stack then followed Paul. Josh and Scotty finished picking up and walked to the elevator bank.

"You'd better watch it—that's MacMillan you just knocked on his ass," Scotty warned Josh under his breath. Josh was puzzled and looked it. *"MacMillan,"* he said loudly, jerking his thumb over his shoulder in the direction of the company logo on the wall behind them.

Josh looked from the logo to the empty corridor where the founder had passed. "Oh, *that* MacMillan," he said.

CHAPTER 9

BILLY could not come into Manhattan every evening, so Josh was frequently on his own after finishing the workday at MacMillan Toys.

His job itself was going far better than Josh had expected, his knockdown of the guy who owned the company notwithstanding. At first, it had seemed certain to Josh that he would be discovered to be an imposter. He had begun his career without a clue as to how a business operated, and despite his considerable experience with Dungeons and Dragons and an occasional piece of wholesome educational software, he had despaired of mastering the mysteries of entering data from handwritten sales order sheets into the company's computer system.

But with a few days' practice and the patient help of Scotty, Josh soon progressed from panic to a mild state of boredom with the routine in the Data Processing Department. *How do grownups stand the thought of doing the same thing over and over for years?* Josh wondered.

Josh mastered the business of shaving without bloodshed and was soon an old hand at getting to and from work, surviving there, and managing all the little incidentals—meals, clothes, getting ready in the morning—that he had never had to deal with when he had been at home with his family. . . .

That, of course, was the problem. His mother had sounded so worried, so sad, on the phone. Before, his parents hadn't paid that much attention to Josh, or so it seemed to him. And he had done his best to escape their company and avoid their instructions whenever he could. Now what he wanted the very most was to be able to return to a world that he not only had taken for granted but hadn't particularly liked.

And was he really going to be able to do that? Would he actually get another chance to grow up gradually, or would he be stuck forever only being big?

It would be at least a few more weeks until he and Billy heard from the City about carnivals. Even when they did, would they really be able to find Zoltar? Would Zoltar change him back if they did find him?

Josh spent his evenings in his hotel room, surrounded by the debris of the candy, pizza, cookies and potato chips that he consumed for dinner. He jumped when a door slammed down the hallway or a drunken shouting match ensued outside his door. He endlessly watched the three working channels of the battered television chained and bolted to the floor. Then he would sleep, just to make it all go away.

One morning near the end of his second week at MacMillan Toys, Josh had just settled into his desk, turned on his computer, and finished arranging his input sheets for the morning's work when his name and Scotty's were called. A clerk with a stack of envelopes was working his way up the center aisle of the department. Josh stood and followed Scotty over to the clerk. They were each handed one of the envelopes.

"What's this?" Josh asked as they walked back to their desks.

"Payday," Scotty answered. "Your first, isn't it?"

Josh tore open the envelope and looked at the short folded piece of paper inside in astonished disbelief. "A hundred and eighty-seven dollars and thirty cents," he exclaimed. It was more money than he had ever *seen* in one place at one time. And it all belonged to *him*.

"Yeah, they really screw you, don't they?" Scotty commiserated.

That evening, Josh stayed late at work. After everyone else had gone home, he phoned Billy. "This is Mr. Simmons, Billy's math teacher, Mrs. Kopeche," Josh intoned. "I wonder if I can have a word with him about this evening's assignment." He covered the mouthpiece with his hand and chortled as he heard Billy's mother summon him to the phone.

"Billy, it's Josh. I told your mom I was Simmons. You'll have to make something up to tell her."

"Yes, Mr. Simmons," Billy said, not missing a beat. "No homework tonight, just study for tomorrow's test?"

"Listen, I was sitting at my desk this morning and one of the guys came along and handed me a *check*."

"I understand what you're saying."

"Billy, it's for a hundred and eighty-seven dollars. I've been here for ten days and already I'm rich."

"Uh-ha."

"Billy, what the hell do I do with this thing?"

"I'll come in to see you tomorrow after school, Mr. Simmons," Billy said, and hung up.

The next afternoon, Billy and Josh waited in line at the bank around the corner from MacMillan Toys—fidgeting. When it was their turn, Josh stepped to the counter and signed the back of the check, as Billy had instructed him, and pushed it over the marble surface to the teller. She took a few additional chews on her gum as she looked at Josh with a bored frown. "How do you want it?" she asked.

Josh stooped down to Billy. "She wants to know how do I *want it*," he whispered. Billy cupped his hand over Josh's ear, whispered back. Josh straightened, announced his answer: "A hundred-dollar bill, eighty-seven ones, and three dimes," he told the teller nonchalantly.

Outside the bank, the friends abandoned their businesslike decorum. Josh fanned the bills in his hand

and whooped, performing an impromptu war dance on the sidewalk.

"Look at that," Billy shouted from his perch atop a garbage can. "It . . . is . . . absolutely bee-yew-tee-full."

Josh stopped, regarded his friend. "Billy, do you know what we are going to *do* with this?"

"What?" Billy said, hopping down to the sidewalk.

"Absolutely everything!" Josh told him.

Josh's room at the St. James Hotel was completely transformed. It was covered with Silly String, which the boys had sprayed from the four cans they bought. Wrappers of food from the four major junk food groups littered the floor and overflowed the wastebasket—insofar as it could be said that they'd actually been put in the wastebasket. It had been the center of a somewhat haphazard basketball game.

Josh sported a T-shirt that announced I'M WITH STUPID. It had seemed the right thing to buy after Billy put on his new glasses, which came with their own eyeballs popping out of the frames on slinky coils.

Josh took a final shot with the Silly String, holding the can to his mouth and pretending he was blowing lunch all over Billy.

"Baaaarf," he said, providing sound effects.

"Too gross!" Billy said. "And besides, I may actually do it." He clutched his stomach and rolled over, leaning toward the wastebasket.

"I'm never going to eat again," Josh announced.

"It was okay until we had the pork rinds," Billy sympathized.

"Nah," Josh said. "It was the boat ride." The memory of the ever-so-slight weave of the Circle Line was just too vivid. To cover his nausea, he spurted the last blast of Silly String at Billy. "What's that drink called again?" he asked.

"Mango fizz," Billy reminded him.

Even then he could still taste the tangy sweet goodness. A grin crossed his face. He picked up the whoopee cushion they'd bought at the tourist place in Times Square. A wonderful blast emitted from it, echoing against the bare walls of the dingy room.

"We sure had fun, didn't we?" Josh asked.

Billy reclined against the dresser and gazed happily at his best friend. "Yeah, we sure did," he agreed.

Josh tried to sleep, but long after Billy had left, he was still tossing uneasily. There was a rumble in his room, and then a groan. With a sinking feeling, Josh realized that it was *his* stomach that rumbled and *his* voice that groaned. It didn't matter whether it was the pork rinds or the boat ride. He felt awful. Even the comforting blast of the whoopee cushion couldn't console him.

Bent nearly double with the ache, he crept out of bed and stumbled to the door of his room. He opened the door a crack. For once, the hallway was empty. Cautiously, he crept out into it on bare feet, clutching a handful of coins in one hand, his stomach with the other. He deposited some of the coins and punched in a very familiar eleven-digit number. He stretched the phone cord as far as it would go, just managing to get it inside his room. He slid down to sit on the floor by the door and listened to the phone ring on the other end.

"Hello, is this the Baskin residence?" he asked when his mother answered. He was speaking as brusquely as his sore stomach would permit. "Well, I'm conducting a consumer survey," he continued. "We were wondering that kind of medicine you give your family when they're sick."

He paused, waiting for the answer. "Well, for a stomach ache, like from eating a lot of junk food," he supplied.

She told him.

"I see," he said sagely. "And how often do you give that?" he asked. He nodded, feeling better already just from hearing the sound of his mother's voice. "Every four hours? That much? Does it taste real bad?" he asked. "Okay, okay. That'll do." He listened, not wanting to hang up. "What? Oh, no, I don't have any more questions. Thanks. You don't know how helpful you've been." Then, reluctantly, he said, "Bye." She disconnected.

Josh lowered the receiver and looked at it for a moment. "Night, Mom," he said. Painfully he rose, reached around the corner, and hung up the phone.

He slipped into his trousers and sneakers, donned his leather jacket, and headed for Broadway to find a late-night drugstore.

CHAPTER 10

O n Saturday morning, fully recovered from his stomach ache, Josh stood at the plaza at Fifty-eighth Street and Fifth Avenue. He gazed at the window of F.A.O. Schwarz. He didn't have an awful lot of his paycheck left to spend, but he still had a full day to enjoy and this was a good place to enjoy it. In the window, a small sailboat floated placidly upon a pond of glass. A brightly painted train circled the pond, puffing smoke. A menagerie of stuffed animals surveyed the scene from cotton candy clouds above.

"Josh!" a man yelled. Startled, Josh spun toward the voice. He saw a man frantically chasing a little boy, who was, in turn, chasing a sheepdog, leash trailing behind, which had apparently escaped the grasp of a mink-coated woman. Josh grabbed for the sheep-dog's leash when it neared him. He stopped the animal with a firm tug and handed the leash to the waiting—and embarrassed—owner. Then, following the man and the other Josh, he entered the store.

The whole place, it seemed, was in motion. On one side, music boxes sang and jack-in-the-boxes popped and bobbed. On another, a man was demonstrating small balsa airplanes, which looped gloriously and then returned to him, boomerang-style. In front of Josh, a giant musical clock rollicked with mechanical toys, which danced the quarter hour.

A boomerang plane looped toward Josh. The boys near Josh grabbed for it—hoping, this time, to keep it from its return trip. The youngster immediately in front of Josh grabbed highest. Josh could see that he might actually reach it.

Josh acted quickly. He shoved the kid aside and grabbed for the plane. The plane caught a gust from the air conditioning. It soared just beyond Josh's reach. Swiveling, Josh chased it down the crowded aisle, jostling astonished customers. Finally Josh lunged upward, stretching as far as he could reach. As he clutched the plane firmly, one foot caught the edge of a Pogo Ball and he lost his balance. He sprawled triumphantly, mid-aisle, grinning. He'd caught the plane.

On the second floor, Josh had to wait about fifteen minutes for his turn to use the Laser Tag set. He could see that the kids ahead of him were really amateurs. He'd get them! When it was finally his turn, he was paired with an older kid named Mark, about fifteen. Josh slid into the vest, and, before Mark fastened his vest, Josh had escaped down the hall. The whole store was infused with the familiar incandescent blue of the castle of the Evil Ice Wizard. Josh ducked behind a life-sized stuffed giraffe, glancing between the beast's legs for a sign of the Wizard's approach. A blur of stringy white beard told him the moment was upon him.

Stealthily, Josh backed out from under the giraffe's tail and into a teepee, shooting at the Wizard as he went. *Pyeew! Pyeew!* he cast the thermal bolts at Mark.

"Missed! You missed!" Mark taunted. "And I got you now!"

Thinking quickly, Josh squeezed out the back of the teepee. There had to be a way! He rounded the teepee, but Mark was nowhere to be seen. Josh stood up and looked around. There, across the aisle, was a gigantic Lego display—just the sort of place an Ice Wizard would hang out. Crouching behind customers, Josh cased the area. He was so intent on finding Mark that he was completely unaware that Mac MacMillan was watching him—closely, carefully, silently—from a vantage point near the service desk.

Suddenly, Josh thought he spotted Mark. He stood to his full height and raised his weapon for the kill, only to find himself looking in a mirror!

"Ha!" Mark shouted from behind him. "I fooled you with the old mirror trick—and now you're going to get it!" *Pyeew Pyeew!* Josh's vest lit up brightly, telling the tale to all. He was done in. He'd been defeated by the Evil Ice Wizard. Again.

Clutching his heart, he stumbled weakly, unable even to lift his own weapon for retaliation. He fell to his knees, eyes riveted to his nemesis. His weapon clattered from his grasp. "Beware the Demon!" he moaned. His eyes shut a final time. Then he issued his death roar and fell to the floor.

He was great and he knew it. Josh's eyes sprang open, and he began laughing until he noticed the feet on the floor by his head. They were wearing fashionable loafers and argyle socks. At the ankles, Josh saw gray flannel slacks with tailored cuffs and sharp creases. Josh followed the creases to the man's waist. When he looked up further, he found himself staring into the all-too-familiar face of the Big Boss—MacMillan himself.

"You work for me, don't you?" MacMillan asked mildly, regarding Josh with frank curiosity.

Josh sat straight up. "Uh, yes, sir, I do," he answered nervously, for the first time uncomfortably aware of his own childishness.

"Thought so," MacMillan said. "You here with your kids?" He offered Josh a hand. Surprised, Josh accepted it and stood up. He unfastened the Laser Tag vest and handed it and the weapon to a child waiting impatiently by his side.

"Uh, no. Just looking around."

"Me, too," MacMillan told him. "I come here most Saturdays." He looked around, studied Josh for a moment, and then decided to confide in him. "Can't see this on a marketing report."

"What's a marketing report?" Josh asked.

"Exactly," MacMillan said. He began walking slowly along the aisle. Josh followed him like a puppy dog. "Tell me, what do you think of this thing?" Mac-Millan asked, pulling a large box from the shelf.

"Oh!" Josh said, eyes gleaming. "Stanley Cup Hockey set! I love that—only . . ." He caught himself, aware that his childishness was showing again.

"Only what?" Mac asked.

"Only that the pieces don't move," Josh finished.

Mac tilted his head and looked more closely at his newest employee. "What do you mean?" he asked.

"Well, in the old set, you could move the pieces up and down the ice," Josh explained. "Now they just spin. It was more like real hockey the other way. How come they changed it?"

"I don't know," Mac told him. "But I know you're right and I know the sales are down and I know I didn't know why they were down until you told me. Let's see if there's anything else you can tell me, young man—Jason, it is, right?"

"No, sir, it's Josh. Josh Baskin."

"A name I won't forget again."

"Thanks, Mr. MacMillan," Josh said.

"Call me Mac, Josh, won't you?"

Josh nodded numbly. Grownups still didn't make much sense to him, but as he walked through F.A.O. Schwarz with Mac, it became clear to him that *he* made sense to Mac and that Mac actually wanted to know what he thought.

"See, the Starfighters are good, because you can change the pieces around. I don't like the Galacticons, because you just get one robot and it *doesn't* come with a vehicle."

"I see," Mac said, and Josh had the feeling that he really did see.

"Plus, they can't go underwater. Now, with the Starfighters . . ."

Josh was startled by the sound of a musical note that came from beneath him. He stopped abruptly and looked down. He found himself standing on a giant-sized keyboard. When his foot hit the middle C, the note was played. A grin crossed his face. He put his other foot on E—then E-flat.

"Hey, neat!" he exclaimed. "Look at this. . . ." Josh skipped across the keyboard, carefully walking through the opening phrase of "Joy to the World." Mac smiled, watching him. Next, Josh jumped back and forth lightly, producing a note progression that was the familiar left hand to "Heart and Soul."

"Piano lessons?" Mac asked.

"Three years," Josh answered. He'd never seen much point in all the time spent on them, either, until now. He became more sure of his steps and picked up the beat a little. Mac's smile became a grin. He reached out his right foot toward the keyboard and tapped the C three times: "Heart . . . and . . . Soul." Startled, Josh looked up at him, almost losing his own rhythm, but recovering successfully.

"Me, too," Mac said sheepishly. "Every day after school." He stepped onto the keyboard and continued the melody to Josh's bass. "And I never had more fun with it," he said, echoing Josh's own thoughts. Together, the two of them tapped their way through the entire song, grinning broadly throughout the performance, even through the occasional errors they made.

When the song finally came to an end, Josh leapt off the keyboard. That made room for Mac's dramatic left-footed arpeggio running the entire length of the keyboard.

Not surprisingly, a small crowd had gathered around the music makers, and there was scattered applause at the finale. Somewhat embarrassed, Josh and Mac bowed and then continued, without consultation, toward the electric train area.

"What division do you work in, Josh?" Mac asked, putting his arm across the young man's shoulder.

CHAPTER 11

There was a new denizen in the executive suite at MacMillan Toys. His office was spacious, multiwindowed, and thickly carpeted. The paneled walls were lined with shelves filled with toys. The new walnut desk gleamed. The telephone console on the desktop had enough buttons to launch a satellite. Next to it lay a remote controller for the TV-VCR-CD discreetly stored in a cabinet built into the wall near the office's back door.

The door opened. In stepped the newest addition to MacMillan's executive ranks, accompanied by his best buddy, Billy Kopeche.

"Wow!" Billy said with unabashed awe. "It's like Christmas in here."

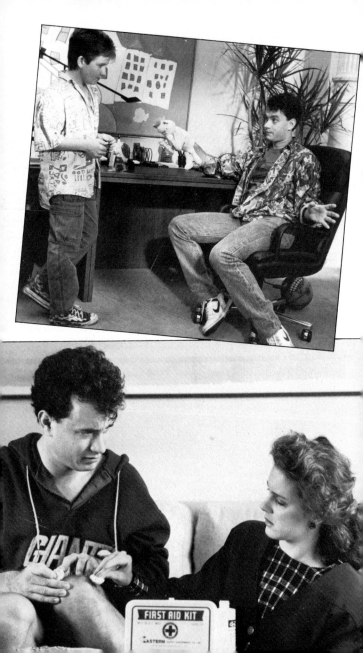

Billy wandered over to Josh's desk and began fiddling with the buttons on the phone, watching lights flash, listening to three dial tones at once.

"Vice president!" he intoned. "That means like if the president dies you get to take over for him, right?"

"Naw," Josh said. "They got a million of 'em." Josh fiddled with his necktie, trying to straighten it out. Now that he'd gotten shaving down pat, the adult world had thrown something else at him—the executive look.

Billy took hold of the top of Josh's high-backed desk chair. He sniffed the fresh leather. "This is the real thing, you know?"

"I know," Josh said. "I got to be careful not to get sticky stuff on it, I guess."

Billy gave the back of the chair a gentle push. The seat spun noiselessly. He pulled it away from the desk. It rolled smoothly on castered feet. Billy sat in the chair. He sank deeply into it, sliding on the smooth leather. He propped himself up with his arms and sat up straight. He looked out over his friend's office with frank envy.

"So what exactly do they want you to do?" he asked.

"I'm supposed to think a lot," Josh told him proudly.

"Suckers," Billy said.

He leaned back in the chair, tilting it to his liking. He propped his feet up on the desk casually. With his left hand, he reached for the phone and began stabbing at buttons randomly. While waiting for the imagined response, he picked up a pencil and stuck the eraser end in his mouth, holding it as if it were a big cee-gar, the kind a vice president would smoke. He puffed imaginary smoke rings and watched their upward progress in the air. When the mogul's phone call was finally answered, Billy was brief and to the point. "Henderson!" he said gruffly. "You're fired!" He slammed down the phone and leaned back in the chair, totally content.

"Yeah, I got to get some cigars," Josh agreed. "That'll make all the difference."

"Hey, what's this?" Billy asked, pressing a button. The door hiding the entertainment console slid open silently. Billy's jaw dropped. "A TV set!"

"Actually," Josh explained, "it's a monitor hooked up to cable." He tried to sound cool, but he didn't fool Billy. "And a VCR!"

Billy shook his head in wonder. He fiddled with the buttons on the remote controller. *Gilligan's Island* came into focus. "You're the luckiest guy I know," he said.

But all was not sweetness and light among the inhabitants of the executive suite. Two of Josh's colleagues, Susan Lawrence and Paul Davenport, took the opportunity to discuss the firm's newest vice president while they were supposed to be observing a dozen five-year-olds in a focus group for their newest brainchild: Pillow Fight.

The children had each been armed with a set of foam rubber boxing gloves of elephantine proportions, perhaps three feet in diameter. The test market researcher had carefully informed them how the gloves were to be used. But before the explanation was complete, the children took matters into their own gloved hands. One child chose an unsuspecting peer to bash mercilessly.

"A week!" Paul exclaimed. "Vice president and he's only been here a week!" His envy was poorly masked by anger.

"Two, I think," Susan corrected him. "They say he came from Data Processing. Maybe he—"

The bashee rose to her feet and counterpunched her attacker. The test market researcher tried to remove one of the two from the mêlée, but by then, four others had joined in on the fun.

"Wait. Let me think," Paul said, ignoring the fracas that had broken out among the kids. "I've got it! He's out of his mind. MacMillan, the old bastard, has completely lost it now."

Five of the children ganged up on the one who had thrown the first punch. Four others were batting one another randomly. Of the two remaining children, one climbed onto a child-sized chair to shout instructions to the combatants and the other stood in a corner and cried, his wails only barely audible above the shouts in the free-for-all. The test market researcher waved his arms, fruitlessly trying to get the children's attention.

"I hear he's got Bob's old office," Susan hissed, her mind totally focused on the biggest problem at hand.

Paul shook his head in dismay. "There's got to be a reason," he said. "Something like this doesn't happen without a reason."

The two sat sullenly staring at the floor, unable to think of anything else unpleasant to say. A bell rang, indicating the end of the fifteen-minute designated period for the focus group. Paul and Susan stood up automatically. Paul glanced again at the pandemonium. A sweet-looking little girl wearing a smocked dress, white socks, and Mary Janes delivered a roundhouse punch to one of her peers, knocking the boy flat on the floor. His face turned a furious red, and tears began rolling down his cheeks.

Paul waved his hand at the hapless test market researcher. "We should take some of the stuffing out," he concluded decisively. He and Susan left the room.

"So," Billy told Josh, filling him in on the events at George Washington since he'd left. "They want to play spin the bottle, but old Shirlee says she doesn't want to play. So David calls her a chicken." Billy snapped his wrist, launching a musical Frisbee. As it spun across Josh's office, it began emitting musical notes, rather like a wind chime.

"Like it?" Josh asked.

"Neat," Billy said. "It's much better than that stupid game from the stupid television show. Anyway, so Shirlee goes, 'I am *not* a chicken. I just don't want to play.' "

"I'll bet," Josh said. He caught the Frisbee and returned it. "Old Shirlee is too—"

Josh's office door opened. Miss Patterson, his secretary, entered the room. She had difficulty masking her surprise at the mess she found. The floor was littered with games and toys. An intergalactic space station had been set up in one corner. She nearly tripped on the scattered pieces of a board game in front of

Josh's desk. Some of the interlocking blocks of MacMillan's Kid City had been made into an Old West cavalry fort. The remaining blocks were spread on Josh's desk.

"Uh, sorry," Miss Patterson said when she interrupted. She picked her way carefully across the office and moved enough Kid City blocks to make space for the papers she'd brought in. Then, as quickly as she could, she left Josh's office, ducking the musical Frisbee as she went.

"So David goes, 'You are *so* a chicken. I bet you never even made out.' And *she* goes—"

Once again their conversation was interrupted. Josh's intercom buzzed. "I guess that's for you, huh?" Billy asked.

Josh nodded. He stepped gingerly over to his desk and picked up the phone. "Yeeees," he said in a deep, very grownup voice. "Oh, sure. Great," he said a few seconds later. He hung up and turned to Billy. "Mac wants me," he explained. "He's the boss."

Billy shrugged. "I gotta go anyway." He dropped the Frisbee on the floor and hefted his book bag to his shoulder.

"Oh, wait," Josh said, looking through the stack of papers Miss Patterson had brought. He pulled out a maroon folder with a sheaf of typewritten pages in it. "She did your geography report," Josh said, offering the folder to Billy.

Billy gaped. "No!" he said incredulously, but accepted the sheaf of papers.

Josh leaned over to him and whispered, "That's

what this whole place is like. You don't do *anything* yourself."

Billy shook his head in amazement.

"So how are things at home?" Josh asked, shifting the subject.

"Compared to this?" Billy looked around at the collection of toys and games—in this enormous playground where Josh got everybody else to do absolutely everything for him. "Give me a break," he said. Resignedly, he slipped his arms through the backpack straps and left.

CHAPTER 12

THE next morning, Paul sat at the breakfast table in his kitchen. Susan puttered at the stove behind him. The morning news droned from the television set on the counter by the window. Neither Paul nor Susan paid any attention to it.

The counters in the kitchen were filled with the latest—and most expensive—in kitchen equipment: a food processor, a juicer, a coffee maker, a microwave-convection oven. The pots hanging from the baker's rack affixed to the high ceiling were copper sheathed, imported. Susan, wearing her wrinkled clothes from the previous day, spooned instant coffee into mugs, stirred briskly, and put one on the table in front of Paul. She then sat down next to him.

"Did you check Mattel?" he asked.

"Nothing," Susan answered. In fact, she'd spent hours the previous afternoon getting in touch with old friends in the toy business, now at other companies, to see if she could find out anything about MacMillan's *wunderkind*, Josh Baskin.

"What about Coleco?"

"Zero."

"A nephew, maybe?" Paul asked.

"I thought of that, too," Susan said. "But we were there when he knocked Mac down. They didn't know each other—for sure."

Absentmindedly, Paul picked up the milk carton and poured from it into his coffee mug. His preoccupation with Josh's meteoric career was so intense that he barely noticed when the cup overflowed. "Well, he can't come from nowhere, Susan," he said, setting the milk carton down in the brown puddle on the table. "Nobody comes from *nowhere*." He rested his arm in the puddle. "Hasbro?" he asked.

"*And* Fisher-Price and Worlds of Wonder. I've called everywhere. The guy comes from Data Processing."

"Terrific," Paul said, and then noticed the mess he'd made of his shirtsleeve. "This is just terrific," he snarled. "Everything's really terrific." Fuming, he turned to the television. Something there had caught his attention.

". . . as the Justice Department broadened its probe into insider trading with the additional arrests of seven men from Maxwell, Crawley,'' the newscaster was saying.

Silently, Susan mopped up the coffee and milk puddle from the table, watching the television while she worked. Paul stepped into his bedroom and returned, putting on a clean shirt while the news story continued. It provided something else of common interest to them, beyond Josh's promotion.

''. . . It marks the first time the insider trading scandal has extended to the bond market area,'' the newscaster told them, while the picture showed a group of pin-striped men and women being led from their skyscraper offices in handcuffs. The alleged perpetrators averted their eyes from the interfering television cameras.

''See, it's all terrific,'' Paul snapped sarcastically at the television. ''Now they're arresting businessmen! The new American crime''—he turned to Susan—''trying to earn a living.'' The detectives hustled the day's catch into a waiting paddy wagon.

In disgust, Paul snapped off the television set and returned to his coffee.

Susan made herself another cup of instant coffee and poured milk into it. She set the container back on the table in front of her. She drank her coffee in silence, keeping her thoughts to herself. Her eyes never focused on the grainy photograph on the side of the milk carton. Otherwise, she would have seen the bright smile and curly hair of a twelve-year-old boy named Josh Baskin, recently abducted from his family's home in New Jersey.

HAVE YOU SEEN THIS CHILD? the advertisement inquired.

Later that morning, at ten-thirty sharp, the door to Mac's office closed to announce the start of the weekly line review meeting, which was attended by all upper-echelon executives, vice presidents and above. Each member of the staff reported progress on development and market research of new products. Sales patterns on existing products were evaluated as well. It was every department chief's opportunity to shine—or go into eclipse.

Josh sat between two men he'd met quickly the day of his promotion. One was named Bill and one was named Jim, but he couldn't remember which was which—and the fact that each wore an identical Paul Stuart suit, Brooks Brothers shirt, Countess Mara tie, and Gucci shoes didn't help. Well, one's tie was red-on-yellow. The other's was yellow-on-red. They made Josh think of Tweedledum and Tweedledee, but after a quick glance around the room, he realized that the sorting problem was more serious than just telling Jim and Bill apart. In fact, Susan, the sole female, was the only executive Josh could easily distinguish by name.

Paul was speaking. He stood easily at the side of the conference table, next to an easel, which showed a large bar graph professionally produced in four colors. He used a telescoping pointer, tapping it on the graph frequently for emphasis. His monotonic presentation was punctuated by the emphatic tapping of the pointer.

Mac slumped slightly in his chair, listening to Paul's

presentation. Susan listened faithfully. Josh leaned forward from the leather sofa where he sat and picked up the prototype of the toy Paul was presenting.

". . . The focus testing showed a solid base in the nine-to-eleven bracket with possible carryover into twelve-year-olds," Paul droned. He flipped the chart on the easel, revealing a new and more promising bar graph.

Josh turned the prototype in his hand, looking at it quizzically. It was a skyscraper, sort of, with a joint at about the forty-third floor. He manipulated the upper stories to see what was supposed to happen. The sides of the building dropped away, flopping to ground level and revealing robotic legs underneath. The upper stories, unmetamorphosed, were apparently supposed to be the robot's head. Josh wrinkled his nose. He looked carefully at the robot's legs, but he couldn't see any joints in them. He tried to make them move. They didn't budge.

". . . when you consider that Gobots and Transformers pulled a thirty-seven percent market share," Paul said, tapping his new chart again, "and we're targeting roughly the same segments."

Josh tried turning the top of the building again, but nothing happened at all. He could replace the sides and make them fall away, but that was it.

"I think we could see about a quarter of that, which . . ." Paul paused for effect. "*Which*," he repeated, "would be about one fifth of our total revenue of all of last year." He beamed proudly. "Any questions?"

Several seconds of silence filled the room.

Josh turned the toy upside down. "I don't get it," he said to no one in particular.

Everybody in the room stared at him, including Susan, and especially Paul. There was a slight but audible gasp.

"Just what exactly don't you get?" Paul asked from between clenched teeth.

"It turns from an office building into a robot?" Josh asked.

"Precisely," Paul said.

"Well, what's fun about that?" Josh asked in genuine wonder.

A murmur filled the room. Paul's eyes narrowed to slits.

"If you'd read your industry breakdown," he said, barely above a hiss, "you'd see that our success in the action-figure area has climbed from twenty-seven percent to forty-five percent in the last two years."

"Oh," Josh said. There was an audible sigh in the room, and all eyes remained on Josh. He shrugged. "I still don't get it."

Mac sat up and leaned toward Josh. "What don't you get, Josh?" he asked with interest.

"Well, I mean a robot—that's old," Josh said. "Couldn't it turn into something else, like a bug or something?"

Paul's eyebrows arched. "A *bug*?" he asked, astonished.

"Yeah," Josh continued. "Like this big prehistoric insect thing, maybe with really huge claws that can pick up a car and just crush it like that." Josh closed his fists tightly, almost able to feel the disintegrating vehicle in his own palms. Billy would like that, too.

"A prehistoric transformer?" Bill—or maybe it was Jim—asked from the sofa next to Josh.

Josh nodded.

"Interesting," Mac mused.

Paul got the intensely unpleasant feeling that he was losing his audience—and losing his brainchild.

"So the building turns into a monster?" one of the other officers said.

"I guess," Josh agreed.

"Say, we could put out a whole species!" another officer chimed in.

"Yeah, you could hatch them out of houses," Josh said, expanding the idea.

Still sitting at his desk, Mac nodded. A smile crossed his face. "Maybe the eyes could blink," he said, and then he grinned broadly.

And maybe they could emit death rays to young upstart pipsqueak vice presidents, Paul thought to himself. *I know just where to begin.*

The day had not gone well for Paul. At six-thirty he sat in his own Interior Decorator Neutral living room, clutching a crystal glass. The ice cubes jangled in his spasmodic grasp.

"He's vicious," Paul hissed to Susan, sitting opposite.

"He's not *vicious*," Susan contradicted him.

"Don't kid yourself, Susan," Paul warned. "That man is a killer."

Susan recalled the genuine curiosity on Josh's face

in the meeting. "All he said was that he didn't get it," she reminded him.

"Didn't *get* it!" Paul echoed. "He tried to eviscerate me, Susan. He went for my throat! And he drew blood—right from the carotid. Did you see Mac-Millan's face?" The color rose in Paul's own face as he recalled his humiliation at Josh's backhand slap.

"Uh-huh," Susan said. In fact, she hadn't missed a thing at the meeting that morning. Not a thing.

CHAPTER 13

Josh and Billy trailed the real estate agent into the spacious SoHo loft.

"It's quite a unique space," the agent said, eying the pair carefully, choosing her pitch cautiously. "The lines are so clean, and you don't get any of the partition quality you find so often in lofts. Good schools in the neighborhood, too, Mr. Baskin. I'm sure your son will be happy. Right, Bobby?"

"Billy," he corrected her.

She nodded absently and continued. "Brand-new bathroom," she announced, sweeping her hand to the left. "Modern kitchen." She led them to the right. "European-style, with American ingenuity." She began to enumerate the charms. "There's a trash compactor, and—"

Billy's eyes opened wide. "We'll take it," he declared.

A few days later, a large moving van pulled up to the curb in front of Josh's new home. The sign on the side of the truck read: GORDON RENTS—EVERYTHING IN HOME FURNISHING, JUST A PHONE CALL AWAY. The driver climbed down from the cab, examined the front of the building, and buzzed the intercom. "Baskin?" he asked when a muffled voice came through the aluminum grille.

A water balloon struck the sidewalk in response.

Dear Mom: They said I could write you and let you know I was okay.

That was true enough, Josh thought. He was okay. He was more than okay. His new apartment was a sort of dream come true. He especially liked the pinball machine he'd bought. And the bunk bed so Billy could sleep over. And his skateboard. And the train set. And . . .

So far, they've been treating me fine. I've got enough to eat . . .

The food was great, too. He just wished he'd taken more French. Sometimes the menus were hard to understand.

. . . and I'm perfectly safe.

He was safe, if one overlooked how far he'd climbed onto the ledge to get the kite that had gotten stuck on somebody's TV antenna. But it was a neat kite, made to look like a glob monster. It had really taken off. He couldn't let it get ruined.

. . . They say I'll get out of here in about a month.

If the lady at Consumer Affairs wasn't lying.

. . . In the meantime, it's a lot like camp.

Especially the day when he'd taken part in a focus group, only he'd been the counselor, not a camper. He'd been surrounded by eighteen preschoolers all testing Pogo Balls at the same time. Little kids could be incredible brats sometimes.

. . . I watch TV and even get outside once in a while.

The day at the football game had been just about his favorite. The Giants won by intercepting a pass and returning it for a touchdown—fourth quarter, eighteen seconds to go. His dad would have loved it.

. . . I know you miss me, but try not to worry. I think this experience might even be good for me.

Especially since he'd gotten the black satin Yankee jacket for Billy. Sharing was good for everybody. He'd bought himself one, too. One that fit him now.

. . . I love you and Dad and Rachel very much, and I know I'll see you soon.

He closed his eyes to try to picture his parents. It wasn't easy to bring their faces into focus. It was almost as if he weren't their son anymore. How could he be? He was a grownup now.

. . . Your son, Joshua.

He looked at the tickets for the Knicks game on the desk in front of him. He had to leave in a minute. He was meeting Billy at the Seventh Avenue entrance.

. . . P.S. I stopped biting my nails.

Josh folded the letter and put it into the envelope. He'd mail it on the way to Madison Square Garden.

CHAPTER 14

"**L**OOK at that!'' Josh shouted excitedly, pointing up the block in the direction from which he and Billy had come. When Billy turned to study their route, Josh ducked into the door of Servalot's Men's Formal Wear and squeezed the door shut behind him. In the background, a bell tinkled. Josh peeked around the corner between the doorpost and the display window and watched his baffled friend turning a slow circle in front of the store, trying to figure out where Josh had disappeared to. Josh jumped onto the low platform of the display window. There, framed by the crooked elbow of the morning-coated mannequin in the window, he inserted his thumbs into his mouth to spread his cheeks wide; pushing his eyelids upward with his index fingers, he made a hideous face at Billy.

"May I help you, sir?" asked an unperturbed salesman from behind Josh. Josh let his hands fall to his sides and dropped back down to the sales floor.

"I need to rent a tuxedo." Josh leered as if expecting the stranger with a yellow tape measure looped over his shoulders to understand what an *incredible* joke that was.

Billy stepped throught the door, walked up to Josh, and speared his friend's ribs with a upward jab of his elbow. He regarded the salesman benignly. The salesman looked from Josh to Billy. "Any particular occasion?" he inquired.

"His company is having a party," Billy answered.

"I see," the salesman said, not seeing. "Well, then, you'd probably want something simple. Maybe a shawl collar with . . ." He turned to respond to a whispered question from another salesman. "Excuse me a moment," he told the friends.

"Why can't I come?" Billy took up the thread of a previous discussion with Josh, glancing up at him.

"I told you," Josh replied, looking down. They walked across the showroom floor and stood studying a mannequin, the arms and neck of which were canted at improbable angles. "The party's just for people in the company, and customers. Besides, you wouldn't understand anything that was going on."

Billy regarded him through narrowed eyes. "I could be your assistant. It would be neat."

Josh circled the mannequin. It was clad in a powder-blue tux in crushed velvet. He grabbed it by the lapels. "Listen, pal. I'm takin' over around here, see." He released the lapels, stepped back. "That . . ." he told Billy, waving his hand from the head to the foot of the figure before them, ". . . would be neat. What do you think, Billy?"

"I like it."

The salesman rejoined them. "Uh, usually that type of tuxedo is popular with students," he said dubiously. "Senior proms and—"

"Look at this one!" Billy called. He had dashed to a full-length mirror where another customer was modeling a pearl-gray cutaway. "What kind of tuxedo is this?" he asked the customer.

The salesman scurried into the conversation and steered Billy a few feet off. "It's not a tuxedo. It's a morning coat."

"Hey," Josh called to them from across the store, pointing excitedly into a showcase, "I've got it!"

The massive displays of MacMillan toys on the stage and around the walls looked vaguely out of place amidst the faded nineteenth-century splendor of the Grand Ballroom of the Waldorf Astoria Hotel. Among the formally attired MacMillan employees and buyers assembled in the triple-balconied room for the company's annual spring-line promotion, life-size, costumed versions of Mitor and Gwendoline and other MacMillan dolls and action figures roamed, distributing canapés.

Paul and Susan surveyed the throng from a post near

the buffet. Paul was resplendent in a black single-breasted tuxedo, Susan elegant and stylish in a deep blue watered silk gown. George Malone of the marketing department faced them, completing a small circle. Paul stared over George's shoulder at the crowd so as not to miss out if something more important than their own conversation occurred.

"Oh, come on, George!" Paul focused on him for a moment. "You can't sell to the parents; you sell to the kids." He looked back off into the distance.

"I disagree," George said.

"Listen, you hit them at seven A.M., while their folks are still asleep. Then you get them good and jacked up for a few hours so that by ten they're ripping the house apart." He dropped his gaze to George again, leaned toward him significantly. "It's *timing*, George. You want that parent to wake up hearing little Jennifer screaming 'Puppy-pal, Puppy-pal.' "

Susan had been studying the content and manner of the conversation. She frowned thoughtfully. A familiar laugh erupted behind her. She turned her head to watch MacMillan separate himself from a knot of guests a few feet away and head for one of the bars. It was an invitation to wander off. She murmured an excuse and trailed after Mac.

She heard Mac place his order as she stood next to him at the end of the bar. "Scotch. Neat."

He was taking a sip of his drink, when he noticed her over the rim of his glass. He lowered it and smiled.

"I love your tux," she told him, stroking one of his lapels.

He seemed puzzled. "I think it's pretty much the same as the waiters' in this mausoleum," he observed diffidently.

Susan threw her head back in a gale of laughter. He narrowed his eyes. She stepped closer to him and described a circle on his sleeve with her outstretched finger. "Have you decided what you're going to do on the Danberry line?" she importuned.

"Not yet."

"Well . . ." She drew the word out, lowered her voice, and plunged on with the commercial. "I think if you got everyone's input up front—I mean right at the very beginning . . ."

"Susan," he said gravely.

"What?" She smiled up at him.

"Have a drink."

"What?" she said uncertainly.

"Have a *couple* of drinks," he said, toasting her with his. She was now frankly baffled, her brows furrowed. "It's a party," he explained, then turned and walked away.

Susan trailed thoughtfully in MacMillan's wake, passing the point where Paul continued to hold court. ". . . and with the exchange rate down there . . . their money falling, even against the dollar, you make out like a bandit." Paul regarded his audience conspiratorially as he pontificated. "I get two housekeepers and a cook for five hundred bucks a month. Now, where else are you going to . . ."

Susan moved away. She stopped at a pillar near the

entrance, leaned there, and surveyed the scene. The noise in the great room subsided. As if on cue, the crowd turned toward the main entrance, stage left of the ballroom's giant proscenium. There stood Josh, leaning casually on a white enameled cane, white silk top hat cocked at a jaunty angle.

He was clad from head to ankle in a white satin cutaway.

The suit was embroidered along the lapels and trouser seam with a sequined profusion of green and red curlicues reminiscent of the handwork on the frock of a toreador. Gleaming white patent leather toes protruded where razor-creased trouser legs broke. Adjusting a gigantic snow-white bow tie in the starched collar of his white-on-white shirt, Josh strolled jauntily into the hushed room.

From across the dance floor, Mac followed the gaze of the crowd. He looked puzzled at first, then he smiled tentatively. Finally, detaching himself from the group with whom he had been talking, he threw his head back and laughed uproariously. The titters, stiffled guffaws, and whispered remarks in the room grew to a crescendo as Mac continued his frank and obvious display of admiration for Josh's costume. Mac handed his empty glass to a passing waiter, strode across the room to Josh, placed his arm across the younger man's shoulders, and boomed out, "Glad you could make it, Josh." He pulled his head back to survey Josh, arm still in place. "Glad you could make it."

After the commotion of Josh's entrance had subsided, Susan rejoined Paul and spent most of the evening at his side as an observer.

Paul wouldn't waste any conversation on her when there were important people around to impress.

As the evening wore on, Paul's martini intake made him increasingly pugnacious. "The guy's a goddamn knockoff artist," he informed Halloran of the Personnel Department, who didn't care. "*Amphibian*?," he snorted. "That's G.I. Joe with gills, packaged with plastic seaweed."

Susan eavesdropped on the nearby conversation between Josh and Mac. They had spent much of the evening huddled together, chatting animatedly. Others had drifted over to join in, Susan had observed, only to stroll off when the conversation hadn't turned to a topic to which they could contribute.

"My oldest brother told me it wasn't true when I was five," Susan heard Mac confide to Josh. "When my mother found out, she almost beat him within an inch of his life."

"Well, I figured it out myself," Josh bragged in reply, "because the chimney was too small for *anybody* to get down."

Josh moved off to the buffet. Mac headed for the bar. Susan touched Paul's elbow. "Excuse me," she said. "I'll be right back." He didn't notice. She followed Josh to the food.

Josh lifted up the skirt of the table to see what was underneath. Finding nothing of interest, he dropped the cloth and plunged his finger into the salmon mousse. He eyed the alien substance on the end of his finger. "What do you suppose this glop is?" he asked the man next to him. He flicked the stuff onto the floral centerpiece.

The man chuckled. "So what do you do?" he asked.

"What do I do about what?" Josh asked. The man strolled off.

Sterno cans guttered under chafing dishes. A server in a tall white toque noisily sharpened a carving knife, then applied it to a roast steaming beneath an infrared lamp. Josh watched him with interest.

Susan sidled nearer. She stood next to Josh, facing the room while he studied the trays and bowls, looking for something edible. "All the same people having all the same discussions," she said, not looking at Josh. "It's like they cloned some party in 1983 and keep replaying it again and again every year."

She turned to him dramatically. "I *loved* your ideas on the Squeezy Doll line," she confessed breathlessly.

Josh looked at her. "Oh. Thanks." He poked at a mound of liver pâté with the tongs from the shrimp bowl. "Why do you suppose they have cat food?" he wondered out loud.

"They had such clarity," Susan continued.

A waiter replaced an empty tray with one containing toast points surrounding a crystal bowl of black bee-bees in clear Jell-O.

"It's beluga," Susan told him, following his puzzled glance.

"Oh, yeah," Josh said. He spread some of the caviar on a piece of toast, tossed it into the air, and caught it in his mouth. He chewed reflectively. Suddenly his eyes went wide and he convulsively sprayed the food back onto the tray and over the surrounding area. "Uggggh!" He grabbed a martini from the tray of a passing waiter and tossed off half of it with a gulp.

He spat that out on the carpet.

"Are you all right?" Susan asked anxiously. Josh wheezed. "Do you want some water?"

Josh nodded enthusiastically, his eyes wide. "I don't understand why they don't have anything to eat or drink at this party," he sputtered ruefully.

"Listen, I have a company car . . ." she whispered, glancing to where Paul continued to hold forth to one of his colleagues. "Let's get out of here."

"Sounds good to me," Josh croaked. He headed toward the entrance, retrieving his hat and cane from a chair near the door.

"Terrific," Susan murmured, and followed.

They descended the staircase to the main lobby, walked through it, and left through the revolving door. "Just seeing somebody in the office," Susan told him, "you don't really get the chance to know him."

"Right," Josh agreed.

They crossed the street and walked down the block. Her sleek gray company car was parked in front of a fire hydrant. "Neat car," Josh told her across its roof.

She paused. "Do you want to drive?"

"I'd love to, but I'd better not." Susan unlocked the door of the driver's side, inserted the key into the ignition, then reached across the compartment and opened the passenger door. She started the engine.

Josh tossed the cane and the hat into the back seat, jumped in, and pulled the door closed. The automatic seat belt silently moved along its track above the door and snapped Josh safely into place. "That's the coolest thing I ever saw," he announced in awestricken tones.

She pulled away from the curb, turned onto Lexington Avenue, and headed downtown.

Josh explored the wonders of the center console. He locked and unlocked the doors with gratifying clunks. He opened and closed the windows individually, which was easy, then simultaneously, which was harder. He flickered the lights on the visor's vanity mirror experimentally. It was great.

Susan glanced over at Josh as she drove, puzzled by his absorption in extra-cost options.

"The office is a hard place to *really* develop an acquaintanceship," she told him.

"It sure is," Josh replied, discovering automatic station search. It was fast, too. The car was filled with classical music, hard rock, and "all news all the time" in quick succession.

"It's hard in a business situation. I mean, there's that invisible line." She cast a sidelong glance at Josh to find him staring across an invisible line, in fascination at the orange instrument display behind the steering wheel. ". . . and even if you're attracted to somebody . . ."

"ET, phone home," Josh shouted, snatching the

mobile phone from its mounting as they stopped for the light at Gramercy Park.

"Is there, ah, somebody you have to call before . . ."

"Hello, op-er-ay-tor, give me five-oh-nine," he sang. "If they do not aah-ahn-ser, give me back my dime." He paused, listening, then, "No. I'm in a *car*. I'm actually talking on the telephone in a car." He paused again. "A dollar and a half a minute for this nonsense!" He mimicked the operator incredulously, holding the phone at arm's length. He hastily replaced the instrument in its cradle.

Susan pulled away from the stoplight. They were nearing the loft building area where Little Italy spilled into SoHo. "Actually, I'm feeling a little vulnerable right now," she confessed, staring straight ahead.

"That's the good thing about Superman," he observed. "He's *in*vulnerable. Except, of course, for Kryptonite."

Josh flicked open the automatic locks with his left hand and opened the passenger door a crack with his right. "Your door is a ajar," he heard. "Your door is ajar."

"Dumb computer," he remarked. "*My* door *is* a *door*. Hey," he shouted, glancing out the window. "We're on my block. That's my building right *there*." He pointed excitedly out the window.

She pulled to the curb. "Oh?" she said, sounding surprised.

She had had to forgive Halloran for the Judy fiasco to get Josh's address out of him.

"I'd love to see where you live, Josh," she said, turning off the ignition and facing him.

"Hey, come on up," Josh said expansively. He was being a quiz show emcee. He opened his door the rest of the way, retrieved his cane and hat from the back seat, and climbed out. Susan joined him on the curb. "I've got a whole bunch of neat toys that we could have a lot of fun playing with," he said in confidential tones.

She took his arm, looked deeply into his eyes. "You do?" she asked huskily.

"Oh, yeah." And I've got a whole *box* full of extra batteries for them.

"Unh-huh," she managed in response.

They entered the building and rode up to Josh's loft in a slow elevator big enough for a truck. His hat was at a silly angle. He twirled the cane like a drum major. "Have you always lived alone?" Susan asked as they approached the door.

"No. Not always."

"Well, it's hard, coming off of a relationship," Susan told him. "It hurts. There's no way around it. The pain. The sleepless nights." Josh studied her as he dug around in unfamiliar pockets for his key. "But that's what they invented Xanax for. Right?"

"Is that some kind of new action figure?" he asked her with interest.

She looked at him strangely. "Are you all right now?" She asked, staring deeply into his eyes.

"Yeah, I'm fine," he replied, staring back. Then, shrugging, he fit his key into the lock.

"I don't know if we should do this yet," she said, evincing belated doubt.

"Do what?" he asked.

"Well, I mean, I like you, and I *want* to spend the night with you . . ."

"You mean, *sleep over*?" he asked incredulously.

She was surprised. "Well . . . yes."

"Okay," Josh decided at last, "but I get to be on top."

CHAPTER 15

"**Y**OU *live* here?" Susan asked as she stepped tentatively into the loft. Josh's apartment seemed to be a combination toy store, pinball arcade, and gymnasium more or less arranged around a central bunk bed island complete with large inflated palm trees and plastic pink flamingos.

"Yeah, ain't it something?" Josh beamed. "I designed it myself."

Josh deposited his hat, cane, and bow tie on the floor and reached down to untie his shoelaces. Rising, he attempted to drop-kick his patent leather shoes through the door into the kitchen.

Left made it. He thrust his arms straight into the air, signaling the field goal. Right was wide. He x-ed the failure in the air with palms down, arms swinging at the elbow.

Josh shrugged out of his tails and dropped them atop the pile of other costume parts on the floor. He snapped his suspenders contentedly and then strode across the polished wooden floor to a gigantic Pepsi machine between the windows on the opposite wall. In stocking feet, he slid to a stop at the side of the machine and kicked it sharply with his heel.

The machine emitted a familiar loud *kah-choonk* as a can of soda dropped into the delivery bin. Josh snatched the can up, popped its top, and chugalugged thirstily. "What did you say that junk on the buffet was?"

Susan was still standing near the doorway, arms at her sides, staring at him. He regarded her. "Say, would you like a Pepsi?" he asked, offering her the side of the machine with a wave of his arm. "You won't need any money or anything. I rigged it myself."

She walked up to him solemnly. He reared back and kicked the machine again, plucked the can from the bin, and handed it to her.

She walked over to a nearby card table and reached out to pick up a model spaceship there. "Don't," Josh told her, alarmed. She withdrew her hand and looked at him, puzzled. "Glue's not dry yet. It's got to go a full twenty-four hours."

Susan looked at him intently. "Sorry."

Then she noticed something over his shoulder in the corner. "Is that a *trampoline*?" she asked in amazement.

"It sure is," Josh replied proudly. He sailed his

empty soda can in the direction of a wastebasket across the room. It missed. He walked over to Susan. "You want to try it?"

"Oh, no. I couldn't possibly . . ."

"C'mon. It's a lot of fun."

"No, I can't."

"Sure you can. It's easy." Josh took her by the arm and steered her toward the trampoline.

"My shoes," she protested.

"Take 'em off," Josh countered.

He hopped onto the trampoline, took a couple of experimental bounces, then extended his hand to Susan. She hesitated, reached down to pull off her high heels, then climbed up onto the trampoline.

They were standing face to face. Josh was bouncing joyfully while Susan tried to keep her balance. Susan held her shoes in her right hand. With her left hand she hiked up her skirt to free her legs for jumping.

Josh noticed this appreciatively.

"I feel so silly," she told him.

"Give me your shoes." He tossed her high heels across the room, then leapt from the trampoline to the floor. "Now, really jump."

"I can't."

"Go on." She rose several inches from the taut surface, then landed with knees bent, stopping altogether. "No," Josh shouted, smiling, "jump!"

Susan tried a few serious jumps and wound up several feet in the air. "Wow!" she exclaimed.

"That's more like it."

Soon, to her astonishment, Susan found she was

having a marvelous time. She was grinning and bouncing around like a lunatic, like a kid. . . .

She stopped, slid to the floor. Josh was nowhere in sight.

She tiptoed to the other side of the room, where she could hear him through the closed bathroom door. He was noisily brushing his teeth. She rushed to the light switch by the hall door and flicked it off.

The room was now bathed only in the romantic fluorescent glow of the outsized Pepsi machine. Susan walked over to the bunk and slipped her evening gown over her head. Climbing into the lower bunk, she pulled the comforter up to her chin.

It was gaily printed with Star Wars characters.

She watched the bathroom door intently. It opened. Josh, clad in bright yellow pajamas, stood framed in the doorway. Suddenly, he let out a whoop and ran swiftly in her direction. *Oh, my God,* she thought momentarily, *what if I've gone home with some kind of maniac?*

Josh vaulted into the upper bunk, the bed shuddering with the force of his landing.

He hung his head over the edge of his bed and smiled down at her. "That's one of the things I like about being on top," he explained.

She smiled at him uncertainly. He extended his closed fists down to her. "Pick a hand," he said. Susan hesitated, then pointed at his left hand. He opened it. It was empty. Josh withdrew his arms, extended them down to her again. "Try again." On the third try, he opened his hand and a small green object fell to her mattress. She picked it up. It was a glow-in-the-dark green plastic ring. It looked like a prize from a cereal box. She looked from it to Josh's upside-down face in wonder. She slipped it on.

They chatted happily for a long time about everything that popped into their heads. Josh talked a lot about his childhood. It seemed to Susan that his recollections of his youth were particularly sharp and vivid. She was especially moved by Josh's story of the time he had wanted to melt into the ground when he hadn't been allowed onto some contraption at a carnival because of his height—and had been ejected from the ride in front of a beautiful girl named Cynthia.

She wondered as they talked if Josh's ingenuousness and imagination had made MacMillan favor him, rather than some dirty trick he had played behind Brad's back. Come to think of it, she, too, felt attracted to Josh; she was inspired by him as Mac also seemed to be, to recall her own childhood.

She was recounting a memory of her adolescence when Josh's head and arms again appeared over the edge of his bunk. "You know what I like most about all this?" He gestured to include the whole loft. Susan smiled up at him. "I like it that no grownup can come in and tell us to go to sleep when we're having a good time talking." He disappeared back into the top bunk.

Susan resumed her story. "That Friday we sat on Cheryl's porch, waiting for them while it got darker and darker. Tina saw the first one and then I saw another, until soon the whole yard was shining with fireflies. I'd never seen anything so beautiful.

"We spent two hours chasing them up and down the street. I caught about a hundred and put them in a big glass jar with holes punched in the lid. I put them right next to my bed, and they glowed all night like tiny little stars.

"When I woke up the next morning, do you know what I saw?" She paused. "Do you know what was really in that jar?" She stopped again. "Dead bugs. They were all brown, with lots of legs and little antennae. I made my mother dump them down the toilet and washed my hands, and I never caught another firefly again. Never. Isn't that silly?"

The top bunk was silent. "Josh," Susan called softly. "Josh, are you asleep?" She rolled over and stared in the semi-darkness at the glowing plastic ring on her finger until she fell asleep.

CHAPTER 16

"**H**AVE fun last night?" Paul asked. He gripped the steering wheel of his BMW tightly. The rain pummeling the roof and the rhythmic swish of the windshield wipers masked the tremors of anger in his voice.

"Sure," Susan answered lightly, watching the suburban Connecticut roadside pass by.

"You left pretty early," he continued accusingly.

"I gave him a ride home." She stared out the passenger window of the car, wishing she were someplace else.

"Did he enjoy it?" Paul asked snidely.

"Don't be ridiculous," Susan snapped. *Someplace else, anyplace else—no, not any place*, she thought.

"Yup. That's me. Mr. Ridiculous," Paul joked

weakly. "Just a silly old guy with silly old notions about seeing you after the party. And that's what I felt like when I saw you leave—Mr. Ridiculous. Or was it just ridicule?"

"I really don't feel like going tonight," Susan said, expressing her discomfort.

"What do you mean? They're *your* friends."

The thump of the windshield wipers metered the moments of silence.

"I know," Susan admitted without enthusiasm. Idly, her fingers grasped the automatic lock switch on her armrest. She clicked it forward. With a gratifying *clunk*, her door locked. She clicked it backward, releasing the lock.

"You don't feel like seeing your old friends anymore?"

The double meaning did not escape Susan. "That's not what I said," Susan protested. She hated having Paul put words in her mouth that way. She continued fidgeting, clunking the switch back and forth, now with the metronome of the windshield wipers, now with the rhythm of her heart.

"Do you have to fiddle with that thing?" Paul snarled.

Surprised, Susan looked at the switch. She had been completely unaware that she was toying with it.

Back in Manhattan, the rain began to subside. Mac MacMillan sat in his office, feet propped on his desk comfortably. A bottle of J&B, now half full, occupied a corner of the desk. Mac held a crystal glass in his hand, staring at the amber liquid, swirling it around in the glass. He took a sip and then placed the glass on his desk.

He leaned back and stared at the glass and the bottle, isolated in the spot of light on his desk from the green library lamp, a relic from his first office. It was the only thing he'd kept from that office when his budding company had made its first move. He'd returned all the other furnishings to the Salvation Army, where he'd gotten them in the first place.

He glanced at his window when a gust of wind whipped a wave of raindrops against it. The deluge outside blurred the lights emanating from the office towers that surrounded his own. It blurred the whole world—from where he sat. Something was lost, he thought, reaching for his glass of scotch. He withdrew his hand, sighed, and shook his head instead; then he wove his fingers across his waist and stared out at the indistinct world.

There was a knock at his door. Surprised, he said, "Come in."

The door opened, bringing in a stream of light— and Josh Baskin. Josh carried a bundle of papers. He was in his shirtsleeves, a pencil tucked behind one ear. There was a smudge of ink on his shirt, and his tie trailed out of his rear pocket.

"Josh?"

"Yeah. Did I interrupt something?"

"No. What time is it?" Mac asked.

"It's almost ten," Josh told him.

Mac stared at his newest vice president for a moment. "Want a drink?"

"No, thanks." Josh approached Mac's desk with

his papers and, uninvited, slid into the chair facing his boss. He put the papers on the far corner of Mac's desk.

"Me either," Mac said. He leaned forward, putting his feet back on the seventy-five-dollar-a-yard carpeting selected for him by an interior decorator who had no idea what he liked and didn't like. Mac picked up the bottle, unscrewed the cap, and topped off his glass with two more fingers of scotch. He picked up the glass and drained it, wincing as the drink went down. "What are you doing here?" Mac asked when the flame subsided.

"Well, I was finishing the Astroblaster," Josh explained.

Mac leaned back and regarded Josh carefully. "What do you think?" he asked, and then wondered immediately why he'd bothered. Everybody always thought everything he worked on would have a 20 percent market share.

"It's okay," Josh answered simply.

"I know what you mean," Mac snorted. He poured another shot of scotch into the glass. "Astroblaster. Lasermite. They're all the same goddamn thing." He held the glass in his hand and turned it, examining it in the single light. "There was this duck," he said to the glass.

Mac leaned back in his chair, depositing the glass on his desk and picking up the bottle. "It was a little wooden quacky duck," he said, pointing to the bottle. "It had a string on the bottom." He tugged at an imaginary string on the bottom of the scotch bottle. "When you pulled it forward, it kind of waddled from side to side." He tipped the angled bottle from side to side for show. "So one day . . ." Mac continued, sitting up straight and putting the bottle back on the desk. "One day I realized that if you put the head on a hinge—just a little wooden dowel—the beak could peck at the ground when you pulled it forward." Mac's eyes were round and his face suddenly animated. "That's it, see. I had an *idea*." He slammed his hand on the desk for emphasis. The solid walnut of the desk—chosen by the interior decorator with a keen eye for commissions—kept the impact from rattling the scotch bottle or the glass.

Josh remained quiet, watching Mac carefully. Aware of this regard, Mac shook his head and rocked back in his chair.

"I used to be the last one out of here. I turned off the lights every night. Look at that." He gestured toward the window, where the wind had dissipated the raindrops. The city's lights sparkled impersonally. "Nobody stops."

For a moment there was silence, then Mac continued. He tapped a stack of papers on the desk in front of him. "You know what this is?" he asked. Josh shook his head. "It's a report on how to expand the adventure market past the twelve-year-old cutoff point."

"Really?" Josh asked.

Mac shook his head. "You *can't* expand it past twelve-year-olds. It doesn't work."

"Why not?"

"Because you can't keep a kid from growing up." Josh stared at him silently with understanding.

"All a thirteen-year-old boy wants is a thirteen-year-old girl—and I don't know how to build one of those."

The president leaned back in his chair, once again propping his feet on his desk. He hooked his thumbs through the armholes of his vest and focused his eyes on the report.

Josh rose and walked away from Mac's desk. "Good night," he said at the door.

Mac was lost in thought and didn't answer.

Even as he stood in the middle of the playground the following day, Josh couldn't figure out what he was really doing there. Paul had invited him to play handball, and Josh couldn't imagine why. Paul had been mean and awful to him from the first time they'd met—when he'd dumped all the papers in the hallway and knocked MacMillan down.

Paul was decked out in a pair of trim gym shorts with NYAC discreetly printed on the left thigh. His shirt sported an alligator, and his shoes were Nikes. In fact, Josh considered the possibility that everything Paul owned had a designer label on it. Where, he mused, would the alligator go on his boxer shorts?

Josh had on a pair of worn cutoffs belonging to Mr. Kopeche, and his father's Giants T-shirt. It just about covered the shorts. His sneakers also belonged to Mr. Kopeche—whose feet were somewhat larger than Josh's—and the label had been removed as soon as they'd been paid for at K Mart.

"Ever played handball, Sport?" Paul asked, surveying Josh's outfit with a sneer.

"Well, I've played tetherball a couple of times."

"That's nice," Paul said, slipping his hand into a thick leather glove. "Above the line on a serve," he explained. "In bounds to the fence, play to twenty-one." He pulled his protective goggles over his eyes. "Ready?"

Before Josh could answer, Paul delivered the first serve. It caromed off the concrete wall and flew past Josh.

"One-zip," Paul announced. He served again. Josh returned the serve, yowling with pain when he smacked the ball with his bare hand. Paul didn't notice the yell. He *did* notice that Josh's return was out of bounds.

"Two-zip," he declared.

Josh tried his best, but Paul was an experienced player and had racked up eighteen points against Josh before Josh scored at all. Local players hanging around outside the chain-link fence gazed at the carnage. Paul had difficulty hiding his deep feeling of joy.

"Twenty-one to five," he said, whipping his goggles off and smiling expectantly at Josh.

"Boy, you're good at that!" Josh exclaimed in frank admiration.

"Had enough?" Paul asked smugly.

"Oh, no. I'll play again."

"You will?" Paul couldn't imagine that anyone would invite humiliation.

"Sure. That was fun."

Surprised, Paul narrowed his eyes and examined his opponent. Then he shrugged, pulled his goggles down, and tossed the small ball back to Josh. "Fine," he said. "You serve."

With each volley, Josh became more assured. The hard ball's odd hops became familiar, and more and more often, Josh was able to be where it landed. He even learned how to make the ball go where he wanted and how he wanted. He'd always been adept at sports, even though Billy Kopeche regularly beat him at basketball. It didn't surprise him when his game improved. It did, however, seem to surprise Paul. With every point Josh earned, Paul's grin turned from joy to determination, then to a grimace.

Paul took a deep breath for concentration and focal energy. "Eighteen-eighteen," he said. "My serve." He tossed the ball up and sliced his hand through the air, connecting boldly. The ball shot toward the wall, curving viciously. It slammed against the concrete and bounced twice in front of Josh. "Nineteen-eighteen," Paul announced.

"That was under the line," Josh protested.

"What?"

"That was under the line. You said the serve had to go *over* it."

"No, I didn't."

"Yes, you did. You said it had to be above the line on a serve."

"Did not!"

"Did too!"

"Did *not*! Now, give me the ball!"

"You did *too*!" Josh said, fury rising in his voice. He held the ball back and away from Paul.

"Just give me the goddamn ball!" Paul grabbed at the ball.

Josh yanked it away from him. "That's cheating!" he yelled.

"Listen, you little shit—" Paul hissed, charging. He fisted his gloved hand and swung straight at Josh. Josh ducked most of the punch and charged, head first, pounding into Paul's stomach and punching on either side as he attacked. Paul pounded at Josh's sides as well, and then kicked at him until Josh lost his balance. Josh, however, had such a tight grasp on Paul's waist that the two of them fell to the ground together, punching, kicking, scratching at each other like two twelve-year-old boys settling a dispute.

Forty-five munutes later, Josh sat on the couch in Susan's office. He'd changed back into regulation work clothes, but the tale of his lunch-hour mêlée was well evidenced by cuts and bruises. He sat erect, clutching a pillow on his lap so that he could squeeze it if the medicine stung.

She dabbed at the scrape on his cheek with hydrogen peroxide.

"Ouch!"

"Now, sit still," she chided him. "I can't clean the cut if you keep wiggling. Don't be such a—"

"He didn't have to punch me," Josh complained.

"I know." She peeled the backing off a Band-Aid and smoothed it gently on the largest scrape. Then she reached for the bottle and began cleaning the next cut. "He's scared of you," she told Josh. "You don't play his game."

That did not seem logical to Josh. "I tried to play his game, and he beat me up!"

"Now, let me see your knee," Susan said. Josh hiked up his trouser leg to reveal a nasty abrasion. Crouching on the floor, she began working at the cut carefully. Josh winced, clutching the pillow.

"If he's scared of me, then why did he punch me?"

"He punched you *because* he's scared of you."

"That doesn't make sense," Josh said.

Susan finished cleaning Josh's knee. When the Band-Aid was in place, she carefully lowered his trouser leg so it wouldn't put undue pressure on the cut. "He's threatened by you. He's threatened by everyone, actually." She completed the thought, realizing, for the first time, what made Paul run. She drew herself up and sat next to Josh. She took his hand.

Josh looked at her with a little surprise. "So how come you're so nice?" he asked. Susan froze, holding her breath. "You work as hard as he does. And you're not like him."

Susan released her breath and looked away from Josh. "You don't know me very well."

"Sure I do," Josh said. She turned back to him. "And you're one of the nicest people I've ever met."

Susan shook her head in wonder. Never in her life could she remember meeting anybody like Josh Baskin. She sighed in happy confusion. *How do you do it?* she wondered.

For a few seconds, they just looked at each other. Then, ever so slowly, Susan leaned over to Josh and kissed him once, softly, on his sore cheek.

It made the hurt go away.

* * *

Early the following day, she stormed into Paul's office. He made a ridiculous picture, sitting at his desk in a business suit, with a black eye and a Band-Aid on his forehead.

Susan strode right up to his desk and dumped a shoe box on it.

"What's this?" Paul demanded.

"What does it look like?" Susan retorted.

Paul lifted the lid of the box and looked inside.

Susan listed the contents for him. "Shampoo, razor, toothbrush, two neckties—I always hated that mauve paisley one—and your exercise tape. That's what it is."

"Susan," Paul began in the sweet, patronizing voice that was another thing she'd always hated about him.

"I want my keys back," she interrupted.

He stuck his hand into his pocket, pulling out a set of keys. He tossed them across his desk carelessly, so that they slid off the far end and landed on the floor. Susan stooped quickly and picked them up.

"He's only got a few scratches, honey," Paul said. "He'll get over it."

"*This* has nothing to do with him." She was surprised at how true that was.

"Oh, come on. What is this? Your big moment of redemption?"

And that was *another* thing she hated about him. He thought he was the master of snide remarks. "No," she told him. "This is *your* big moment to fall on your ass. Remember? It's good for you."

"Who are you kidding, Susan? He's another link in the chain. First it was Bob Alexander, then Myles, then me.'' The saccharine smile looked comically out of place with the bruise and the bandage. ''Am I missing anybody?'' He was proud of his *coup de grâce*.

Susan shifted her weight to one foot and put her hand on the opposite hip. Her eyes narrowed. ''Yeah,'' she told him. ''You're missing Golding and Thompson and Cochran. So *what*, Paul?'' She was trying to hurt him, and she knew she'd hit home with that.

Taken aback, Paul blurted, ''So what's so special about Baskin?''

Susan put both her hands on Paul's desk and looked him straight in his black eye. ''He's a grownup.''

She righted herself, pivoted on her high-fashion high heels, and marched out of Paul's life forever.

CHAPTER 17

"**H**EY, Josh, check this out," Billy said, pointing to the pizza chef who was flinging a platter-shaped glob of dough into the air. When he caught it on his fists and kept it spinning, the hungry and appreciative audience burst into applause.

The boys were at Asti's restaurant. It was Billy's turn to treat as a birthday present for Josh, who was turning thirteen.

The remains of a double-everything-but-anchovies pizza sat on the table between them. The table was scattered with empty soda cans.

The pizza chef tossed the dough one more time, and when it landed, he deftly split the dough into small balls and tossed them out at the diners. Billy and Josh each caught a glob. The chef then challenged the patrons to throw the dough back at him. He opened his mouth to a gaping hole and pointed. Billy eyed his target and winked at Josh. Winding up, he threw a strike with a submarine delivery. "See, just like Tekulve," he announced, and watched while the astonished chef was nearly choked by the dough. Billy turned to Josh.

"I know what let's do," he said excitedly. "Let's get a *Playboy* and you buy some beers, and . . ."

Josh looked quickly at his watch. "I can't," he said quietly.

"What do you mean?" Billy asked in surprise.

"I have to go somewhere."

"Where?"

Josh realized that, for the first time in his life, there was something he couldn't tell Billy Kopeche. He couldn't tell him because Billy wouldn't understand. He wasn't big enough.

"I got to go meet someone," Josh said, shrugging off the uncomfortable feeling.

"But I got all night," Billy said.

"I know. I'm sorry, but I just told someone. . . ." He tried to think how he could explain it to his best friend. "I just can't right now, Billy, okay?"

The tenor voice of their waiter broke into tune. "Happy birthday to you!" he sang, and then was joined by six other waiters and the pizza chef. Together, they carried a cake brightly lit with candles and placed it in front of Josh as they finished singing the song. Josh looked at Billy and grinned widely.

"And many, many more," Billy announced loudly.

The whole room burst into applause for Josh. He stared at the flickering candles, waiting.

"What are you going to wish for this time?" Billy asked.

Josh couldn't answer that one, either. He took a deep breath and blew out the candles, every single one of them.

Susan paced nervously around her apartment. She'd changed her clothes four times, finally deciding on a comfortable pair of faded jeans and a bulky wool sweater and a white cotton blouse. She hadn't had so much trouble deciding what to wear on a date since she'd been a teenager. Her whole apartment was tidy. She'd been storing things for an hour now, expecting the doorbell to ring at any moment, though it still wasn't time.

She lit the candles on her mantelpiece. She turned the lights down low and put Mantovani on the stereo. Paul had always liked that. She blew out the candles, turned the lights up, and turned off the stereo.

Her doorbell rang.

When she opened it, there was Josh. She took a short, involuntary breath.

Josh looked at Susan when she opened the door. He noticed her hair, her pretty sweater, the glow in her eyes. Suddenly, it was as if he were seeing her for the first time.

A sea wave broke under his heart.

"Come in," she invited him.

"Sure," he said, stepping into her life.

* * *

Later, Josh took Susan's hand. "Ever been on one of these?" he asked, pointing at a roller coaster. They had come to Seapoint Park, a tourist trap on the Atlantic shore in Brooklyn. There were rides and games and fun houses. It was Josh's kind of place.

Susan looked at it warily. "Yeah, but it's been a long time," she said. "I really don't know."

"Aw, come on," he urged. "Then we can get some popcorn, and a candy apple. And I think I saw some Italian sausage!"

"Jo-osh!" she said. "You're positively crazy." He grinned at her. "And I like you that way." She followed him to the roller coaster. It was wild and wonderful, climbing slowly up to peaks with a sporadic jerking of the cars, only to be hurtled smoothly and swiftly downward with a roar. They clutched each other and screamed as one. When the ride was over, they stumbled off.

Josh glanced at the faces of the teenagers who were waiting to get on. It seemed like so long ago that he'd been among them, like them, only too young and too short to ride the Avenger. *Could it only have been a few weeks?* he asked himself. He began counting but was interrupted by Susan.

"Have you got any change, Josh?" she asked.

He fished in his pocket. "I've got some quarters," he said. "What for?"

Susan was stopped in front of an old carnival game on the boardwalk. LOVE METER, the sign said. The dingy glass case housed a mock thermometer with a series of red light bulbs to indicate everything from *Boring* to *So-So* to *Intriguing* and on to *Fabulous*.

There was something familiar about it. Maybe it was just because it was an old-fashioned gimmick. Maybe it was the elaborate ironwork or the faded brocade behind the "thermometer," but it made Josh hesitate.

"Come on, Josh," Susan urged him.

"I don't know," he said with deep reluctance.

Susan took one of the quarters out of his hand and held it up to him temptingly. He relented. He took the quarter in his hand and dropped it into the slot. Then, following the directions, he took the smooth brass handles in each hand and squeezed as hard as he could.

The light bulbs came to life, blinking wildly. Josh released the handles and took a step back, nearly bumping into Susan. They waited, giggling together, while the machine finished its blinking and chugging. Finally, the diagnosis was revealed. *Dangerous*, it said.

Josh glanced at Susan and she returned his look. Their eyes locked. Slowly, Josh leaned forward.

"Hey, did you hear that?" Susan asked. Josh backed away. "It's big-band music over there at the pavilion," she said. "I haven't heard anything like that for a long time. Let's go see. Want to dance?" she asked shyly.

"Dance?" Josh asked as if he'd never heard the word.

"We don't have to," Susan said hurriedly, embarrassed.

"No, it's okay," Josh said. "Let's go."

He took her hand, and they headed along the dimly lit boardwalk toward the pavilion. The band was playing "Chattanooga Choo-Choo." They sang it together as they walked, totally absorbed in each other.

They were so absorbed that neither of them saw the other old carnival game in the dark shadows off the edge of the boardwalk, shoved against the side of the arcade building. In the wood and glass booth, the bobbing head of Zoltar grinned grotesquely. The figure's eyes glowed bright red. As the couple passed, the glow subsided; the bobbing stopped.

"I don't really know how to dance," Josh confessed as they stood on the side of the dance floor, hesitating.

"I'm not very good, either," Susan told him. "I haven't done this in a long time."

She offered him a hand and took him out onto the dance floor. Gently, she placed her left hand on his right shoulder and, with her right hand, took his left. He put his right hand on her back. She smiled up at him and began moving to the gentle music. He moved with her. She drew him close to her, resting her head on his shoulder.

"What were you like when you were younger?" she asked.

"Oh, not much different," he answered truthfully.

"I believe that about you. You know, I've been thinking a lot about you." They danced easily now, having found a rhythm. "It's crazy, though. In the shower, on the phone. I'm thinking about you. You'd think I was a virgin!"

Over her shoulder, Josh's eyes popped open.

Susan went on. "When we were walking out here— along the boardwalk, you know—I kept thinking, what if my hand sweats? Can you believe that? What if my *hand* sweats?"

Josh glanced at his moist left hand, clutching Susan's right hand. Carefully, he removed his right hand from her back and wiped it on his jeans before replacing it. Susan snuggled closer.

"I've never gone out with someone like you before," she said. "With every other man, there was always so much to hide. I don't feel that way with you."

The music stopped then. Josh pulled a few inches away awkwardly. "Susan," he said, his voice cracking.

"What?" she whispered eagerly in his ear.

"I think there's something I better tell you—" he began. The music started again. Susan took him in her arms again, and they began dancing again.

"It's okay," she said. "You can tell me later." She circled his neck with her arms and put her cheek on his chest. He sighed and held her tenderly, firmly, swaying gently with the music.

She looked up at him then. His eyes met hers, and the moment was theirs. He leaned forward and met her eager lips with his.

It was a night of firsts for Josh. An hour after his first serious kiss, he found himself standing next to Susan in the bedroom of her apartment.

Kissing was *one* thing. . . .

While Josh stood immobile at her bedside, Susan shrugged out of her bulky sweater and began unbuttoning the white cotton blouse underneath. Josh watched in fascination, unable to move or speak. He was transfixed. When she'd removed her blouse, she leaned across Josh and turned off the light. He gasped.

As quickly as she'd turned it off, he turned it on.

"You want the light on?" she asked, smiling up at him.

He nodded. "Definitely."

"Good," she cooed.

There she stood in front of him with absolutely nothing covering her beautiful grownup breasts. Somehow, he managed to lift his right arm and reach out to her. Ever so gently, his fingers touched the side of her breast. It was soft; it was warm; it was a *breast*. Quickly, he brought his hand away, staring at his own fingers in disbelief.

A dreamy grownup smile crossed Josh Baskin's face as they collapsed together on the bed.

CHAPTER 18

JOSH emerged from the elevator on the executive floor of MacMillan Toys the next morning with a newfound spring in his step. He carried his attaché case easily. He strode surely, grinning at his fellow officers and employees. He winked at the Sparklettes Water man, who was hefting a five-gallon water jug into place atop a cooler. When the man stepped back, Josh gave him a high five. Startled executive secretaries exchanged curious glances.

Josh swung around the corner toward his office. "Good morning, Miss Patterson," he said brightly. "I'd like some coffee, please."

"But, Mr. Baskin, you never drink—"

"And make it black," he added.

* * *

Nearby, Susan approached her own secretary's desk with a little more difficulty, since she was carrying a very large wicker basket, filled to overflowing with treats. It had a giant white bow on it. Susan placed the basket on Judy Mitchelson-Hicks's desk, but the woman was transcribing a Dictaphone tape and didn't notice the arrival of her boss or the basket.

Susan leaned over, plucking the earphone from Judy's ear.

"Congratulations, *Mrs*. Hicks!"

Judy's jaw dropped. Would wonders never cease?

"My God," she gasped. "It's absolutely gigantic."

On Sunday evening, Susan and Josh stood outside the apartment of Susan's friends the Roses. Josh was going to his first dinner party.

"Do you like this?" Josh asked, tugging doubtfully at bottom of a new sport coat.

Susan regarded him critically. "Wear it unbuttoned," she advised, undoing it herself. "There, that's great," she said, giving his lapel a pat.

After preliminary clicks from its multiple locks, the door opened. Susan's oldest friend, Karen Rose, and her husband, Phil, stood in the doorway, smiling expectantly.

"Karen, Phil, this is Josh."

Both the Roses kissed Susan. Phil extended his hand to Josh. "How do you do?" he asked.

"Nice to meet you," Karen said, grinning knowingly. The phone had been buzzing all day.

Conversation before dinner was easy, casual, and

friendly. Susan noticed that Josh held back somewhat, seemingly a little uncomfortable, but that was natural, since he'd never met her friends before.

At the dinner table, conversation turned to television. "We saw this great documentary about Columbus the other night on PBS," Phil remarked. "I never knew it, but he had a fourth ship."

Josh looked up from his empty dessert plate. "The *Santa Christina*," he supplied. Everyone at the table looked at him in surprise.

"That's right," Bill said.

"But that was only on his second trip," Josh continued.

"You saw it, too?" Phil asked.

"No, I, uh . . ." Josh wasn't sure how to explain. Then he said proudly, "I studied this stuff in eighth grade." That, after all, was true. His dinner companions were clearly impressed.

"Dad . . ." An eleven-year-old boy in the doorway interrupted the conversation uncertainly. He was wearing pajamas and carrying an open textbook.

"Not now, Adam," Phil said gently.

"But you *said*—"

"We've got guests," Phil reminded his son.

Karen leaned over to Josh to explain the interruption. "He's had the hardest time with algebra this year. We've tried tutors and everything."

"Algebra?" Josh asked. Karen nodded. Josh turned to Adam. "Let me see that, Adam," he said.

Adam brought the book over to Josh. He pointed to a series of equations. "I just don't understand," Adam said. "I mean if I take away—"

"We can do this together," Josh told Adam confidently. "Come on. I'll show you." Josh excused himself from the table and followed Adam from the room.

Karen's eyes met Susan's. When the rest of the table stood up to return to the living room for coffee and liqueurs, Susan and Karen tiptoed to the door of Adam's room to eavesdrop. They glanced in. Josh and Adam lay on their stomachs on the floor, the book, paper, and pencils spread out in front of them.

"See how that works, Adam?" Josh asked, unaware of the women at the door of the room. "That's three x plus seven *minus* seven equals twenty-two *minus* seven. *Then—*"

At the door, Karen grinned broadly. "You're right," she whispered to Susan. "He's wonderful."

"I know," Susan replied, smiling to herself.

Billy Kopeche paced back and forth in his room. Downstairs, his parents were snapping at each other, the familiar background noise to almost everything in his home. He sat on his bed and reached for the phone. The cord was stretched to the limit and would trip anybody who tried to cross the hallway, but Billy didn't care. He needed to talk to Josh, and he needed to do it in private.

There was something going on, he was sure. Josh had dashed out of Asti's the week before like he'd been shot out of a cannon. It was okay that he'd had something else to do. Sometimes that happened, but Billy couldn't imagine what it was that could have been so important that Josh didn't even finish his birthday cake.

It had been expensive, too. And worst of all, Josh hadn't called him since then. Something was going on.

He picked up the phone and dialed again. The phone rang and rang and rang. There was no answer.

Where the hell could he be at 11:45 at night?

The illuminated dial of Susan's clock read 11:47. She turned in her sleep, cuddling close to the warmth of Josh's body. His arm encircled her tenderly. Barely moving, he kissed the nape of her neck. His head relaxed back onto his own pillow, and soon he slept, too.

CHAPTER 19

"YOU can do it. I *know* you can!"

Susan's words of confidence rang in Josh's ear. Whatever made her think that he could design an entire line of toys by himself?

Studying the mindless scribbling that filled the yellow legal pad in front of him on his desk, he grimaced. He tore the top page from the pad, crumpled it into a ball, and threw it at the wastebasket across the room. It missed. The latest yellow ejecta rolled across the carpet to join the jumble of other paper wads littering the floor around the wastebasket.

"Nobody knows more about toys in the whole company!" Susan had encouraged him.

That could be true, Josh told himself. But knowing

about toys and knowing what would be fun to play with were a far cry from designing something new, different, economical to manufacture, and most of all, fun. He recalled, not for the first time, that if Mac decided to go ahead with some harebrained scheme of his, the company would spend hundreds of thousands—if not millions—of dollars developing, manufacturing, and marketing it.

What if it bombed?

"All he wants from you is a proposal," Susan had reminded him. "If you come up with the idea, *I'll* handle the marketing!"

What if there was nothing to market? What good would all her expertise be?

Josh took his pen and made a giant X on the fresh page of the pad. He tore that off and threw it at the wastebasket as well. It went in.

That was some progress. His mind was a blank, but at least his aim was improving.

Disgusted, Josh turned off the light in his office. He wasn't actually accomplishing anything anyway. It was time for a change of scenery.

The sailboat and airplane in the window at F.A.O. Schwarz had been replaced by strolling mechanical teddy bears. The clouds above were now filled with bright kites that shifted smoothly in mechanical breezes. In another window, an electrified crane lifted an erector set beam to the top of a skeletal building while helmeted plush toy beavers oversaw the construction.

Josh idly studied the reflection in the window of a

group of youngsters poring over a comic book held open menu-fashion by the boy in the center of the group. He turned to look at the boys directly. Comics had changed a lot in recent years, Josh thought as he walked off down the block.

The old comics in his collection, bought in some cases for several dollars in individual clear plastic slipcases, had poor graphics on cheap paper. The new versions were far glitzier—sharp images on slick paper, better artwork, stories that were at the same time less farfetched and more imaginative.

Josh reasoned that comics had *had* to change in recent years to compete with huge improvements in special effects on TV and in movies and with the interactive nature of the second- and third-generation computer games that competed for kids' spending money. Those games didn't just *sit* there, like a book, however richly illustrated, but *responded* to the user, reacted differently if the user reacted differently. . . .

Comics were now expensive enough and good enough to be sold in bookstores found in every mall Josh had ever been in. They were marketed the same way and in many of the same bookstores that computer game software was marketed.

What would happen, Josh wondered, if you could *cross* a comic book with software—?

He stopped suddenly, then bolted for a subway entrance.

"Depending on what button you push," Josh was saying to Susan as he waved a yellow legal pad excitedly, "a different story appears. See—*you're* the one that's making it up."

They were sitting on the floor in Susan's living room. Josh stretched out his legs, pushed away a pizza carton with his foot, and subsided against the couch front.

Susan hugged her knees. "A living comic book. You *decide* where the action goes. It's sort of like those multiple-ending books publishers have been doing, only much more dynamic and flexible. And the possibilities for graphics!" She released her knees and reached across to grab Josh's hands with her own. "It's just unbelievable." She smiled at him excitedly.

Then her smile faded. She dropped his hands, turned her face to the wall.

"What's the matter?" Josh asked with concern. She shook her head without looking at him. "What's wrong?" He slid closer to her. "You mad?"

She turned to face him. "What are we doing?" she asked plaintively. Josh knitted his eyebrows. "I mean if it's an affair, that's one thing, but if it's something else—I mean not that we have to know right now; we don't—but if we *think* it could turn into something else, then . . ." She paused to study his reaction. "Well, how do *you* feel about all this?"

Josh looked at his notes as if he might be able to find the answer there. "How do I feel about what?"

"How do you feel . . . about . . . me?"

Josh studied her serious expression, his mind racing for a clue as to what could be upsetting her. Then he understood. It was him. She wanted to know if he liked her, if they were going to keep on being friends.

Josh rolled his eyes theatrically, then closed them;

he clasped his hands to his chest, then collapsed to the carpet next to her. Reviving from his swoon, he reached up with both arms and pulled a now giggling Susan into a long, warm embrace.

The next afternoon, Billy Kopeche trudged thoughtfully up the hill a block from home, walking along the side of the street until he reached the crest. Seeing no approaching traffic to interfere, he stepped to the middle of the thoroughfare, dropped his skateboard on the ground, stepped aboard, and shoved off for the long, free ride to his house.

Josh didn't call him anymore. Billy was having no luck calling *him*, and it had been more than a week since Billy had been into the City. It was easy enough to understand how his friend could be busy during the day—pretending to be a grownup, pretending to be working. But what could he possibly be doing all those nights and weekends when he couldn't be reached by phone?

Billy leapt from his skateboard, stamping on its heel as he dismounted. This flipped the board into the air and into his hands so that he didn't have to stoop to pick it up. He stepped over the curb and walked up the sidewalk to the front door, stopping automatically to extract the contents of the mailbox.

Along with a bunch of junk for his folks, there was a large brown envelope addressed to him. The return address of the envelope read DEPARTMENT OF CONSUMER AFFAIRS. Billy whooped, yanked open the door, and, dropping the other mail unceremoniously on the hall table, dashed up the stairs to his room with his prize.

He dragged the hall phone into his room, closed the door, and dialed Josh's office. "I'd like to speak to Mr. Baskin," he responded to the MacMillan operator.

After a minute the operator told Billy, "I'm sorry. Mr. Baskin is in conference."

"Well, tell him I called. My name is Billy Kopeche. K-O-P . . . right. Please tell him it's important." Billy hung up and tore open the envelope. Inside were a covering letter and an accompanying computer listing. He studied the list without seeing it, pacing the floor of his room.

After twenty minutes, he tried Josh's number again. "I'm sorry, Mr. Kopeche. Mr. Baskin is still in conference, but I did give him your message. I'm sure he'll return your call as soon as he can."

I'm not so sure, Billy thought.

After supper that evening, Billy commandeered the telephone again and tried to call Josh at his apartment. The phone rang in the empty loft until Billy grew weary of trying and gave up.

Josh's office was a disaster area, with wads of yellow legal paper and typewritten copy strewn around the room. He sat cross-legged on the floor, staring down at a stack of papers before him. He sported a two-day growth of beard on his haggard face and wore a rumpled shirt with his tie askew. Night had fallen in the canyons around MacMillan Toys, an event that had been no more noticed by Josh than the evening traffic sounds dimly drifting up from the streets.

Susan was seated at Josh's desk, hunched over the pad, where she was scribbling notes. She was stocking-footed and had abandoned makeup; her hair was done up in a ponytail. Despite the dark circles under her eyes, she looked precisely like a schoolgirl bent over her homework.

Now she spoke to Josh without looking up. "Do you have the list of story options over there?"

"Yep," he replied.

"Can I see them?"

Josh looked up from his work toward Susan. When she didn't raise her head, he took a plastic airplane from atop the coffee table and launched it in her direction. The plane looped over Susan's head and curved back toward Josh. She looked up to see the plane swoop by, laughed, and rose to chase after it.

As she passed, Josh grabbed for her ankle, leaning on his stack of papers with his other hand in the process. It emitted a loud musical note.

Susan stopped. "What was that?" she asked. Josh grinned and pressed down on her big toe. Another musical note sounded. Susan collapsed next to Josh, her eyes wide. "How did you do that?" she modified her question.

He shoved some papers aside to reveal a round Plexiglas dome, a maze of wires crisscrossing the circuit board it covered. "Here, put your hand on the dome." She touched it lightly. Nothing happened. "Now, touch my hand with your other hand." She did, and the musical note arose from the dome.

"That's incredible."

"It only works if you touch another person," Josh told her. "Well, maybe it would work with a dog."

Susan touched Josh on the nose to the accompaniment of a sustained musical sound. Josh reached out and touched her nose in return. A second note blended into harmony with the first. Then she kissed Josh lingeringly.

This created a different note altogether.

With a laugh, she rose to her feet and took her coffee cup from the desk. "Want some?" she asked brightly.

"No, thanks," Josh said, returning to his work.

Susan strolled lightheartedly through the office on the way to the coffee room. As she walked past the elevator bank, the doors opened and MacMillan stepped off.

"Working late?" he asked Susan with a smile.

She tried to push her hair into a more businesslike shape. "Yeah. We were just . . . I was . . . getting some coffee." She toasted him with the mug.

"You look good these days, Susan," Mac said appreciatively. Her mind fled in panic to his brush-off at the spring-line bash. Then she realized that the remark was MacMillan's carefree admiration, not a delayed pass reception, so she smiled openly at the compliment. "Real good," Mac said. He studied her, waiting for a response, then moved off down the hallway. "Good night," he called over his shoulder.

The next morning, a freshly shaven and crisply turned out Josh sat at his desk in an office from which the debris of the previous evening had been cleared.

A steaming mug of coffee was at his elbow. He was scribbling furiously on a fresh legal pad.

He glanced up from his writing at the sound of a commotion outside his closed door. "I'm sorry," he heard Miss Patterson shout. "Mr. Baskin can't be dist—"

The door crashed open, and Billy strode in, a large brown envelope tucked firmly under his arm. "Where have you been?" he demanded. "I've been trying to reach you forever."

Josh waved his secretary out. She closed the door firmly as she left.

"Hi, Billy," Josh said without evident enthusiasm. "I'm kind of busy right now—"

"I got the list," Billy headed Josh off, throwing the envelope on the desk. "All we gotta do is call."

"I have a lot of work to do," Josh told him evenly.

"What the hell are you talking about?" Billy shouted incredulously. "This is the *list*."

"Okay. Thanks," Josh said, rising. "I'll call you—"

"You'll call me? I'm already *here*, numbskull. Are you out of your mind, or what? We've waited for this"—he tapped the envelope impatiently—"for weeks."

"I. Have. Work. To. Do," Josh yelled impatiently. Then he sank back into his chair. "Maybe one day you'll be able to understand that."

Billy shook off the condescension. "Who the fuck do you think you are?" he thundered, leaning across the desk.

Josh sputtered.

"You're Josh Baskin, remember?" In frustration and disbelief, Billy turned a tight circle in front of the desk. "You came to *me*," he said, pointing to his own chest, "to fix your report card. You hid in *my* basement when Danny Tobak was after you."

"You don't understand." Josh's voice was more subdued, but he still wasn't yielding the point. "This is *important*."

"And I'm your best friend. What's more important than that?"

Josh regarded Billy evenly from across the vast space separating them. Billy glared back over the chasm.

Suddenly Billy rose, snatched the envelope from the desktop, and stormed across the room to the door, snatching it open. He turned and informed a decidedly uncomfortable-looking Josh, "Just remember: I'm three months older than you are, asshole."

CHAPTER 20

BILLY slammed the door of his bedroom and flung his jacket onto his bed. He banged his desk drawer open against the chair back, shoved the brown envelope into it, and slammed it shut again with the chair back. Striding across the room, he grabbed the walkie-talkie from his bedside table and dropped it into the wastebasket next to the desk. The radio's antenna protruded uselessly from the waste around it. Billy slumped into the desk chair, crossed his arms tightly over his chest, and stared at the antenna, brooding.

After all he had done for Josh, after all they had been through together both before and after Josh got to be big, Josh suddenly had more important things to do than listen to Billy—or to come home.

Josh had completely lost sight of why he *had* a job and was hiding in the city in the first place. And if Josh was going to stiff-arm attempts to help him, Billy didn't want any part of him.

Moreover, as far as Billy was concerned, if being big meant behaving like Josh had behaved, ignoring your family and your best pal, then Billy didn't want any part of being big either.

As if in response to these fugitive thoughts, loud static sputtered from the speaker of the walkie-talkie.

Billy got up, retrieved the radio from the trash tentatively, then walked to the window and looked out toward Josh's window. Josh's *former* window.

Josh's mother was standing in his room, looking over toward Billy. She held the other walkie-talkie in her hand. When she saw Billy, she shrugged apologetically, pointing to the radio with an upturned palm. Billy slid his window open. So did Mrs. Baskin.

"I wasn't sure how to use this thing," she called with a sad smile.

"That's okay," Billy called back.

Mrs. Baskin turned to walk away from the window, hesitated for a moment, turned back. She held up a paper bag for Billy to see. "I baked some cookies. I thought you might want some."

"Oh, thanks." She turned to go downstairs. "Hang on a second," Billy called to her. She stopped. He turned and pulled his butterfly net from its brackets on the wall, backed away from the window to accommodate its long handle, then walked toward the window, extending the net out over the intervening driveway.

"No wonder you boys . . ." Her voice faltered. She composed herself, went on. "No wonder you guys never got any sleep." Billy held the net steady, regarding her. Finally she placed the bag of cookies into the net, as if somehow reluctant to part with it.

Billy retracted the net, opened the bag, and devoured a cookie. "Now, close your window before you catch cold," she said in more official grownup tones, beginning to close her own window.

"Hey," he said. She stopped, looked at him expectantly. "Everything is going to be okay," he assured her with newfound resolution.

She studied him, closed the window, and disappeared from his view. The lights in Josh's room went out.

Billy returned the walkie-talkie to his bedside table. He ambled to the desk. Opening the drawer, he took out the brown envelope and extracted the computer printout from it. Then he dashed from the room.

He had a lot of telephone calls to make.

Josh sat and gazed thoughtfully at the blank screen of the computer monitor on the desk in Susan's dining room. If Billy wanted to get mad at him because he had an important project to finish, then that was just the way it was going to have to be.

He reached down to his open briefcase on the floor and extracted a floppy disk from its interior cover pocket. He turned the disk in his hand, staring at it. Then he popped it into the disk drive of the computer and booted the machine.

The screen before Josh turned an incandescent blue.

He was in the cavern of the evil Ice Wizard, facing his nemesis alone, the floor around him strewn with the twisted carcasses of slain ice dwarfs. . . .

He stood, lifting his jacket from the chair back, and stalked out of the room and out of the apartment.

Josh wandered aimlessly in the streets of what some of his colleagues at MacMillan called the FUES—the Fashionable Upper East Side of Manhattan—until he found himself in Carl Shurz Park. He leaned over the railing overlooking the moving water, which was languid and restless like an ocean of black oil.

To the north, where the Harlem River, the tidal flows from Long Island Sound, and what was called the East River converged at Hell Gate, a square blue light on a buoy bobbed and blinked uncertainly in the night.

Josh had gone home that afternoon for the first time.

George Washington Junior High School had looked diminished and distant as he had arrived. Fallen leaves and debris had swirled on its empty playground. Suddenly a bell had sounded, the doors had burst open, and the playground had come alive with shouting, laughing children heading home on foot, on bikes, on skateboards. They were his friends and classmates. None of them had paid any attention to him.

You do not pay attention to a lonely man hanging around at the fence of a school ground.

He'd walked on to the Little League field. There'd been no game on; it was too late in the year. But two boys about his age—about *Billy's* age—had been playing fungo. One had tossed the ball high in the air, regrasped the bat held in his nonthrowing hand with both hands, and hit up into the descending ball. At the crack of the bat, the other boy had settled into the area where he judged the long, lazy arc of the ball would carry it, then reached up at the last second to catch it with a satisfying plop of leather on leather. Then he'd lazily thrown a bouncing grounder back to the batter so that it could be fielded without a glove. Then the process had been repeated.

The boys hadn't spoken. It hadn't been necessary. They had been together companionably, doing the very most fun thing in the world that they could possibly have been doing.

Josh had roused himself and walked on.

He had gone to the Woodrow Wilson High School. It was to be *his* school next year—maybe. In the parking lot, an obstacle course of orange road cones had been laid out for a driver's ed class. A plain sedan had begun to wobble among the cones as Josh had peered through the chain-link fence, watching from behind a group of students awaiting their turn to negotiate the course. Suddenly, the sedan had veered and sped up, bowling over the next half-dozen cones in its path before jerking to a halt.

"Way to go, Cindy," one of the boys had catcalled. They had all laughed, including Josh.

Then a radiant Cynthia Benson had emerged from the sedan, smiling, her blonde hair gleaming in the late-afternoon sunlight.

Josh had stopped laughing and turned to escape. *If Cynthia can get a learner's permit, she is certainly too old for me*, Josh had thought to himself.

Now he stood watching the blue light blinking over the dark waters and realized that his thought about

Cynthia was absurd. The whole business was absolutely absurd.

He turned and walked out of the park.

"Where were you?" Susan called tremulously as the door to her apartment clunked closed and Josh tossed his jacket on a chair in the hallway. He followed the sound of her voice to the dining room. She was sitting at the table, where a tray of sushi and bowls of rice were illuminated by candles that were well burnt down. She waved a pair of chopsticks uncertainly as he entered the room, her left hand controlled in her lap beneath the tabletop.

"Out," he said evenly, sliding into the chair where his place was set.

"Out where?" she asked after a pause.

"I took a walk."

Susan waited for more intelligence. When Josh busied himself with a bowl of cold rice, she frowned sadly. "Josh, what's wrong?" She set down her chopsticks and followed his glance out the window to the shimmering lights of Manhattan. "What is it?" she asked, fear rising in her voice.

He pushed away the rice and turned to study her for a long moment. "I don't know if I can do this."

She compressed her lips thoughtfully. "The presentation?" she said with evident relief. "It's almost finished."

"That's not it."

"Then what?" she asked, alarm returning. He looked at her steadily. She reached out to touch his arm. "What, honey?" She paused. "Is it *us*?" she asked with dread. When he didn't answer, her voice cracked as she urged, "Josh, tell me what's wrong."

He looked back out the window. "Before I met you . . ." he said, his voice far away, ". . . I was in the Little League." Susan looked at him, her expression changing from fear to puzzlement. "And when I was in Little League, I couldn't wait until I was big enough to be in Pony League."

He turned to face her. "Susan, I'm too *big* to be in Pony League."

Susan saw the real sense of loss in his face, heard it in his voice. "Honey, everyone feels like that. We're all getting older."

"It's not that."

"Then what is it?"

"I'm not *ready* for this." His gesture took in the candles, the sushi, Susan, and the Manhattan skyline.

Susan straightened, understanding supplanting the worry on her face. *This* was not a deal killer. This was something she knew about. "You think *anyone's* ever ready? You think there's some magic moment?"

"Susan, I'm a child," he confessed miserably.

She grabbed his hand gratefully and squeezed, her face brightening. "Maybe if we got away somewhere. Went to the mountains for a few days . . ."

"You don't understand what I'm saying, Susan. I am really a kid. I'm thirteen years old."

She dropped his hand. "And you think I'm not?" she challenged, her self-assertiveness momentarily restored. "You think there isn't a frightened teenager inside me, too?"

"You don't understand." He shook his head sadly. "I thought you would understand."

She closed her eyes. It *was* as bad as she thought. "I swore I'd never fight to keep a man from leaving," she said softly, almost to herself.

"Susan, I went to a carnival. I made a wish on a machine. The next thing I knew, I was a grownup. They made me a vice president before I was allowed to stay out past ten o'clock."

"Why are you doing *this*"—her hands made a constricted gesture—"this way?" Susan asked miserably.

"Look, I know you don't believe me, but it's true." Josh plunged on. "There was this carnival in New Jersey, and I made a wish on a machine. It was called a Zoltar machine. It had a bobbing head like that devil in the old *Twilight Zone* with the guy who plays Captain Kirk. If you got a quarter in its mouth, you could make a wish—and I got a quarter in its mouth, so I won. Or I lost. I got to make a wish. So I wished I was a grownup, and here I am"—Josh showed his palms glumly—"being a grownup."

"Please don't," Susan urged quietly.

"When I went to sleep that night, I was twelve years old. But by the next morning, I was grown up. See, that's what I'm saying. I *turned* into a grownup, but I'm really just a child."

"Fine, Josh." Susan was angry and frustrated and hurt. "You're a child. Look, I don't know what you're trying to tell me, but we've got a really big day at work tomorrow, so I'm going to sleep." She stood up. "Maybe we'll both feel better in the morning," she concluded doubtfully.

* * *

After Josh was asleep, Susan rose stealthily from the bed. She stared down at Josh resting peacefully, his tousled hair fanned on the pillow. She slipped on her robe and crept from the room.

She padded on bare feet through the darkened apartment to the hallway and flicked on the light switch. She picked up Josh's coat from the chair by the entrance, fished his wallet from the inside pocket, and dropped the jacket back to the chair.

Susan almost put the wallet back. Then, resolutely—she *had* to know—she riffled through it. In addition to Josh's MacMillan ID, Josh's uncertain grin flashing in a photo marred by shaving cuts, the wallet contained a ten-dollar bill and two singles and a ticket stub from a Knicks game. In another pocket was a Bergen County library card.

It had Josh's name on it and an illegible signature that looked like his.

The library card was stuck to another card by a wad of bubblegum. Susan peeled the cards apart. The second was a baseball card of Don Mattingly.

Susan studied the baseball card thoughtfully. She had thought that Josh's keen interest in childish things had been professional. But this . . . This was a talisman, an icon. . . .

She continued her search in a different compartment of the wallet. From it she extracted a small oblong of cardboard and read it. Then she sat down wearily in the chair on top of Josh's jacket and stared into the middle distance, her hands clasped around the card on her knees. From time to time, she brought the card up to her face to read it again wearily.

It always said the same thing.

YOUR WISH IS GRANTED

CHAPTER 21

THE next morning Josh was seated at his desk, a preoccupied expression on his face.

Susan studied him and reached across the desk from her chair to hand him the papers she had been reading. "These are the notes in case you want them for the presentation," she said, rising.

Josh took the papers. "Right."

Susan picked up a large portfolio case from the coffee table. "Well, I'll get these set up before everybody comes in." She moved toward the door.

"Great," Josh responded without enthusiasm.

Susan opened the door. She glanced past Josh to the window beyond his desk. "Look, it's raining frogs."

Josh turned to her with a puzzled expression, then smiled. "I love you," she said wistfully.

He closed his eyes, opened them. "I love you, too," he said.

Billy Kopeche scurried into the office, dodging Susan and the portfolio. He stopped before Josh's desk. He glanced at Susan, waiting. She shrugged and walked out, closing the door behind her.

Billy slammed a piece of paper on Josh's desk. "It's right there. Seapoint Park, New York."

A loud buzz erupted from the intercom speaker on Josh's desk. He pushed the bar on the front of the machine down. "Yes?" he asked languorously.

"They're waiting for you in there, Mr. Baskin," came his secretary's voice.

"Thanks," Josh said, then released the bar.

"I'll see you around," Billy said, and stalked out of the room.

Josh rose and trailed behind him, staring at the piece of paper in his hand. He folded the paper, put it into his inside breast pocket, and headed for MacMillan's office.

Susan studied Josh intently from her chair next to the easel set up to the side of the conference table. Josh was standing on the opposite side, tapping with a pointer on a box within the large diagram of their proposal. MacMillan sat at the head of the table.

"It's not a normal comic book," Josh said impatiently. "It's an *electronic* comic book. See, it would look like a comic book on the outside, but when you opened it up, there'd be a flat screen with pictures on it.''

There was a murmur from around the conference table. Josh continued. ''Then when you get to the end of the 'page,' you decide what the character does. If you want him to go into the cave, you push one button; if you want him to fight the dragon, you push another.''

Paul Davenport lounged at the foot of the table, opposite MacMillan. ''I don't understand,'' he said icily.

Susan rose. ''See, there's a computer chip inside that stores the choices. So when you reach the end of a 'page,' *you* decide where the story goes, instead of the writer. That's the point. The kid makes his own decision.'' With that, she looked at Josh strangely. He stared back at her.

MacMillan's voice rumbled from the head of the table. ''Is this possible?''

''Yes,'' Susan answered eagerly. ''In fact, it's a very simple program.'' She turned to Josh. ''Isn't that right?''

''So what happens when you run out of choices?'' Jack Taylor, creator of the Gwendoline doll, asked.

Susan looked at Josh uncertainly, then answered. ''Well, that's the great thing. You can sell different adventures. Just pop in a brand-new disk and you get a whole new set of options.''

''We could market them on a comic book rack,'' Market Research observed.

Josh seemed to decide something. He walked over

to Susan, and whispered, "I'll be right back." Susan stared thoughtfully after him as he left the room.

"How much would the unit cost to make?" Mac asked the critical question.

"Well, our initial figure is around seven dollars," she said, still glancing at the door. She turned back to MacMillan. "Around seven dollars with a retail price of, say, eighteen ninety-five."

"Do you think a kid is going to pop for nineteen bucks for a *comic book*?" Paul scoffed from his end of the table.

"I think a kid . . ." She trailed off, a shocked expression on her face. Why had a *kid* burst into Josh's office that morning? Why was Josh letting her run the presentation?

Where the hell had he gone right in the middle of it?

She glanced around the table with false calm, her eyes settling on MacMillan. "Will you excuse me for a moment?" she asked.

Then she fled from the room.

Susan ran down the corridor to the elevator, wobbling on her high heels as she went. She pushed the call button impatiently, looked at the indicator above the double doors, then sprinted for the stairway.

She burst through the front door of MacMillan Toys. The kid from Josh's office was leaning against a No Parking sign. Susan gathered her composure and strode up to Billy.

"Where is he?" she asked quietly.

Billy shrugged.

She held his shoulders softly in her hands. "Please, you've got to tell me where he's gone."

Billy looked into her eyes intently.

Josh stepped out of his cab at the gates of Seapoint Park, paid the driver absently, and strolled through the unguarded entrance and down the midway.

The carnival looked desolate and deserted, duller somehow in the brighter light of day than under the nightly spell of its own gaudy illumination.

The booths and games were boarded up and padlocked, but Josh strolled toward his destination. The iron arms and belts and gears of rides were just so much industrial machinery, cages emptily halted in suspended animation, abandoned by their tenders and screaming captives alike.

He almost missed the booth near the iron-gated entrance to the game arcade. It had been shoved against the wall of the building and abandoned.

Zoltar looked even more tawdry in the daylight than he had at night. There were cracks and paint chips on his face and along his lantern jaw, tarnish on the coin ramp suspended above his head, faded streaks beneath the dust of his green and purple robes.

Josh stood at the front of the machine, fished a quarter from his pocket, and dropped it into the coin slot. He smiled grimly. It was not so far to reach this time.

The coin stopped at the top of the ramp. Nothing happened. Josh placed one hand on either side of the machine and shook it. Still nothing happened.

Then he remembered.

He stepped to the side of the booth. There he followed the electrical cord to the wall of the arcade and unplugged it.

Then he paused, took a deep breath, and attacked the side of the machine, fists and feet pounding the cabinet.

It was easy to remember his humiliation and frustration of that night. Now they were joined with his ambivalence and current frustration and rose to a crescendo of flailing hands and feet.

He stopped, stepped back from the machine, and rounded the corner to its front. Zoltar's otherwise empty eyes were glowing bright red. The muttonchop-whiskered head bobbed hypnotically. The sign inside the booth lit up: AIM RAMP TOWARD ZOLTAR'S MOUTH.

Josh grasped the control handles and maneuvered the coin ramp into position. The second sign illuminated: ZOLTAR SAYS MAKE YOUR WISH.

Josh closed his eyes tightly, leaned his head back, and wished.

He opened his eyes.

From down the midway, he heard Susan loudly calling his name. "Jo-osh!" The sound rang emptily around the deserted buildings.

He paused momentarily, wondering. Then his resolve returned. It was better to be who you are than to pretend to be someone you are not. Better for the people who knew you and better for the ones who thought they did . . .

He concentrated on the machine's controls. "Jo-osh!" Her voice echoed down the midway.

When the coin ramp was in just the right spot, Josh pushed the button that released the coin. "Jo-osh!"

Her voice sounded closer now. His hands fell to his sides. He waited.

The coin wobbled down the ramp, seemed to pause, then dropped off the end of the ramp into Zoltar's gaping mouth.

The jaws closed soundlessly. A moment passed. A faint mechanical whirring came from the control panel. The end of a small oblong of cardboard was ejected from a slot next to the coin release button.

Susan burst around the corner and rushed up to him. She looked numbly from Josh to the machine, then pulled the card from its slot. The machine went dead.

Susan read the message hopelessly, tears streaming down her face. Then she threw her arms around Josh, hugging him hard, as if she hoped to hold him physically, as if she could keep him from going away—if she could only hold him tight enough.

"Josh, don't leave me," she pleaded through her tears.

"Susan," he managed to whisper, holding her gently, patting her shoulder softly with his hand. "Susan, please . . ." He swallowed. ". . . Please, don't." His voice cracked.

She pulled back and looked up at him. Tears were streaming down his face, too. He fumbled in his pocket for a handkerchief, averting his face.

He was thirteen, and when you're thirteen, you don't cry in front of girls.

Susan understood.

She reached down somewhere inside to find the strength for what she had to do. She would have time to take care of herself, to mend, later. For now, though, she took a deep, shuddering breath and looked at Josh—tenderly, differently. A smile dawned impossibly on her clouded features. Then she hugged him and pulled his head to her shoulder. "Josh, honey . . ." she began.

"I'm sorry," he keened. "I'm so, so sorry."

"Shhhh . . ." She rocked him ever so gently, holding the back of his head against her shoulder with her palm, staring unseeing into the distance. "It's okay," she said, rocking. "It's okay."

They spent the night at Josh's loft. As the sky purpled and reddened into dawn, they climbed into her car and headed for Josh's home, his real home.

Susan parked a few doors up the street from Josh's house. "Which one is it?" she asked.

They were holding hands. He pointed down the block with his free hand. "That one over there." He was excited, eager to go. Susan wished that they could linger, if only for a few more minutes . . . .

She managed an indulgent smile for his happy anticipation of homecoming. He was simply unaware of the hollowness she felt inside.

"You won't even remember me," she told him.

"Oh, yes I will," he said huskily. Then they moved together in a lingering kiss.

Josh opened the car door. He stretched, surveying his home turf spread out gloriously before him in the brightening early-morning sunlight. Then he closed the door firmly.

Susan wiped away a tear, then straightened behind the wheel and leaned forward, unable to believe her eyes. A thirteen-year-old boy was walking away from her car and down the middle of the street toward home. Trouser legs and sleeves bagged on his legs and arms. He stepped right out of his shoes and kept on walking.

On the front steps of his house, Josh turned to her to wave a floppy goodbye with an overgrown sleeve.

As Susan slipped the car into gear, sunlight gleamed momentarily through the glow-in-the-dark green plastic of the ring on her hand.

Then she took a deep breath and started back to the City.

ABOUT THE AUTHORS

B. B. HILLER is the best-selling author of THE KA-RATE KID novels, which were published in conjunction with the successful motion pictures. Her husband and sometime collaborator is NEIL W. HILLER. His short stories have appeared in *The Magazine of Fantasy and Science Fiction*. Among the books the Hillers have written together are the novelizations of SPACE-CAMP and THE BEST TIMES. They live in Greenwich Village with their two sons.